Gabriel came to stand in front of Francesca, every inch of his six-foot-four frame exuding male power and potency.

With him this close, she had to remind herself to breathe. She had to remind herself not to stare at his mouth, not to dream about it crushing hers. Had to remind herself she was a woman of pride and would not resort to marrying a man for his convenience.

But what about your convenience?

The voice of her conscience tapped her on the shoulder like an unwelcome guest at a party. Gabriel's plan was tempting. Seriously, ridiculously tempting. One year of her life and she would be free of the shame of her father's gambling debts. She would have her family home back. It would remain in her possession. It would not be sold off to strangers or turned into a hotel or a grubby casino...

"I need your answer, Francesca. Yes or no."

Conveniently Wed!

Conveniently wedded, passionately bedded!

Whether there's a debt to be paid, a will to be obeyed or a business to be saved...she's got no choice but to say, "I do!"

But these billionaire bridegrooms have got another think coming if they imagine marriage will be that easy...

Soon their convenient brides become the objects of inconvenient desire!

Find out what happens after the vows in:

Sicilian's Bride for a Price by Tara Pammi

Claiming His Christmas Wife by Dani Collins

My Bought Virgin Wife by Caitlin Crews

The Sicilian's Bought Cinderella by Michelle Smart

Crown Prince's Bought Bride by Maya Blake

Chosen as the Sheikh's Royal Bride by Jennie Lucas

Look for more Conveniently Wed! coming soon!

Melanie Milburne

PENNILESS VIRGIN TO SICILIAN'S BRIDE

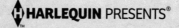 **HARLEQUIN** PRESENTS®

Recycling programs
for this product may
not exist in your area.

ISBN-13: 978-1-335-47829-0

Penniless Virgin to Sicilian's Bride

First North American publication 2019

Copyright © 2019 by Melanie Milburne

Printed in U.S.A.

Melanie Milburne read her first Harlequin novel at the age of seventeen, in between studying for her final exams. After completing a master's degree in education, she decided to write a novel, and thus her career as a romance author was born. Melanie is an ambassador for the Australian Childhood Foundation and a keen dog lover and trainer. She enjoys long walks in the Tasmanian bush. In 2015 Melanie won the HOLT Medallion, a prestigious award honoring outstanding literary talent.

Books by Melanie Milburne

Harlequin Presents

The Tycoon's Marriage Deal
A Virgin for a Vow
Blackmailed into the Marriage Bed
Tycoon's Forbidden Cinderella

Conveniently Wed!

Bound by a One-Night Vow

One Night With Consequences

A Ring for the Greek's Baby

The Scandal Before the Wedding

Claimed for the Billionaire's Convenience
The Venetian One-Night Baby

Wedlocked!

Wedding Night with Her Enemy

Visit the Author Profile page
at Harlequin.com for more titles.

To Emily Payne. You are such a lovely person and I love that you love my books. This one is for you. xxxx

A special thank-you to Franca Poli, who kindly helped me with the Italian translations. *Grazie!*

CHAPTER ONE

FRANKIE HAD COME back one last time to her ancestral home at Lake Como to say goodbye in private. The grand estate with its beautifully manicured gardens would be someone else's home now. Someone else's heritage. Someone else's sanctuary.

She stood at the base of the grand scissor staircase in front of Villa Mancini. The shocking blood-red slash of the SOLD banner across the 'For Sale' sign made something in her stomach grip tight, as if her intestines were caught up in a strangling knot of fishing line. Would the new owner change the villa's name? Turn it into a hotel or a casino? It had been in Frankie's family for four hundred years. Four hundred years of family—generation after generation.

So many relatives.

So many memories.

How could it be possible to lose four hundred years of family history in a game of Blackjack?

Frankie drew in a breath and slowly released it. *You have to survive this.* Now was not the time for a panic attack. Now was not the time for tears and tantrums, because nothing was going to change the fact it was too late to save herself from this shame. It would soon become public. Excruciatingly, humiliatingly public. So far, the press knew very little of her desperate financial situation. She had let it be known she was selling the villa only because she would be moving back to London after two months of nursing her father during his terminal illness. She had called in every favour she could to keep the press away from the truth. But how long could she hope to keep her father's dirty little secret?

She pictured tomorrow's headlines—*Aristocrat heiress Francesca Mancini left penniless by late father's secret gambling debts.*

Frankie had drained her own bank account trying to keep her father's problem a secret for as long as she could. There was nothing left in her trust fund. All the money left to her from her late mother was gone. She had sold her London apartment. How could she let her father's memory be tainted by a gambling addiction he had only acquired in the last few months of his life? His aggressive treatment for brain cancer had changed him. Made him desperate and reckless. She'd foolishly, naively thought her savings would be enough to cover his indiscretions. But her income as a special needs teacher was hardly going to cover debts that ran into the millions.

It was hopeless.

Utterly, heartbreakingly hopeless.

Frankie walked up the left side of the staircase to the front door. She still had her key—the real estate agent hadn't requested it because the new owner would not be moving in until the final paperwork was completed. She unlocked the door and stepped inside the marble foyer but something about the atmosphere told her she wasn't alone. There was a different energy in the air, the villa was no longer cold and empty but alive and breathing.

It had a pulse.

The door to the library on the ground floor was slightly ajar, and from inside she could hear the rustling of papers and the sound of a frustrated male sigh. For a moment, she thought she must have dreamed her father's death and funeral and the debt debacle. A short blissful tide of relief rushed through her, but then she heard footsteps crossing the floor. Strong, purposeful footsteps. She would have recognised that stride even if she were blindfolded. Possibly even if she was deaf.

Gabriel Salvetti opened the library door wide and looked down at her from his superior height advantage. Why hadn't she put on a pair of heels?

Ballet flats didn't quite cut it when she was in the company of the suave and sophisticated Gabriel Salvetti. Not that she ever sought his company—she actively avoided it if she could. Six foot four to her four foot six, he made her feel like My Little Pony facing off a thoroughbred stallion.

His *were-they-black-or-were-they-brown?* eyes met hers. 'Francesca.' He inclined his head in a brief nod that was somehow both polite and patronising at the same time.

'What are *you* doing here?' Frankie couldn't read his expression. She'd always thought he'd make a good spy or undercover agent. Not that his criminal father, brothers and cousins would appreciate that. Gabriel was known as the white sheep in the super-wealthy Salvetti family. The only good apple in a rotten orchard. An orchard so big with deep roots and long limbs and twisted and craggy branches reaching into places no decent person would ever want to go.

But why was he in her house? He hadn't even come to her father's funeral, even though he had done business with him in the past and her father had considered him a friend.

But then she noticed the sheaf of papers in Gabriel's hand and her gut clenched and her heart slipped from its moorings. No. No. No. The words were hammer blows in her head. Surely, *he* wasn't the new owner? How could she bear it? To have the man whose advances she'd spurned four years ago take up residence in her family's home?

Gabriel held the library door open. 'Come in. We need to talk.'

Frankie raised her chin and stood her ground, her mind whirling with what he might want to talk about. 'We do not need to talk. But you need to leave.' Her arm shot out to point to the front door. 'Now.'

'I'm not leaving until we talk. It's in your interests to hear me out.' His expression was enviably calm. As calm as his *adult-talking-to-a-wilful-child* tone. As calm as the silver-surfaced Lake Como outside. Some men took control of a situation by force but not Gabriel Salvetti. He used words economically and curtly. He used stillness and silence as a weapon. He carried with him an aura of command he wore like a second skin.

But the less she thought about his skin the better. She had seen a little too much of it recently. Particularly, a press photo of him at South American beach resort with his latest lover—a blonde model type, whose slim body had made Frankie throb with jealousy. Frankie had inherited her English aristocrat mother's curvy figure and her Italian father's uncontrollable dark brown hair. It wasn't exactly what she'd call winning the genetic lottery.

Gabriel, on the other hand, might not have inherited his family's penchant for criminal activity but he had inherited every one of the Salvetti traffic-stopping good looks. His jet-black hair, chocolate brown eyes, sculpted nose and mouth and tanned and toned athletic build left him with no shortage of female adoration, and consequently, the arrogance to think no woman could resist him.

Which was why Frankie had made such a point of rejecting his offer of a dinner date the night of her twenty-first birthday party. To prove she was immune to him. If not to prove it to him, then to prove it to herself. He'd assumed she would say yes, so she'd said an emphatic *don't-ask-me-again* no, even though a part of her wondered if she had been wise to try and score points with such a worldly man.

And the odd time she had run into him since, she had given him the cold shoulder and hot tongue routine, because, he of all people, was the one person she did not trust herself around. He stirred in her feelings she didn't want to feel. Physical feelings. Feelings and desires and impulses that burned and scorched her inside and out.

Gabriel crossed the foyer to where she was standing and Frankie forced herself to hold his penetrating gaze. Could he see how threatened she was by his presence? His potent, far too attractive presence? *So much for her immunity.* Her body was reacting to his closeness like an ice sculpture in front of a blowtorch. Her skin tightened, tingled, tensed as if anticipating his touch. Even her breasts, hidden behind the layers of her clothes, prickled and shifted in the lace cage of her bra like something too long restrained.

'I can think of nothing you could say that would be of the remotest interest to me.' She injected her tone with a generous dose of scorn. *Eat your heart out, Miss Elizabeth Bennet.* No one but no one could do a cold put-down better than Frankie. She wasn't called an ice princess for nothing.

A half-smile lifted one edge of his mouth, making something in her stomach flip and flop and flap like a torn sail in a stiff breeze. He tapped the paperwork he was holding against his other hand. 'I have a solution to your current dilemma.'

'A…solution?' Frankie affected a laugh. 'I can't imagine how any solution you've come up with would be in any way agreeable to me.'

He shrugged one broad shoulder, his spy face back in place. 'It's an offer. Take it or leave it.'

Frankie could see why he was lethally successful at brokering high-stakes property deals. No wonder he had become one of the wealthiest businessmen in Italy. Even wealthier than his own family, which was saying something. They weren't called the silver-tailed Salvettis for nothing.

She licked her suddenly paper-dry lips. 'Are you offering to…to lend me money?'

'Not lend. Give.'

His eyes held hers in a lock that pulsed with something she didn't want to name. Stubbornly refused to name or acknowledge. But she felt it all the same. Her body betraying her with a slow-moving heat spreading like warm treacle to all her secret places. His deep mellifluous voice with its rich Italian accent always did that to her—made her aware of every inch of her skin, aware of its traitorous desire to get closer to him, even though her rational brain told her, *Danger. Keep away.*

'Give?' Frankie raised her eyebrows. 'Free? No strings?'

The half-smile was back and was even more devastating to her resolve to resist him. She couldn't stop thinking about his mouth and how it would feel to have it pressed to hers. They had not touched each other than a handshake on their first introduction when she was seventeen and a handful of times since, most notably the night of her twenty-first birthday. But it hadn't stopped her wondering what his touch would be like on other parts of her body. Polite nods and handshakes. That's all he had done and yet her body had re-acted, *still* reacted as if he had some strange sensual power over her.

'There are always strings, *cara mio*. Always.' His dark-as-night gaze drifted to her mouth as if he too was having the same wicked thoughts. She took a moment to study him. He was clean shaven but there was enough dark stubble on his jaw to suggest there was nothing wrong with the supply of his virile male hormones. His eyes were fringed with thick lashes and his prominent eyebrows could switch from intimidating interrogation to intelligent interest in less than a heartbeat.

Speaking of heartbeats… Frankie's was currently giving a very good impression of having some sort of medical event. Strings? What strings? What did he mean? And dared she ask him?

He was standing within touching distance. If she so much as reached out a hand she could touch that broad, muscle-packed chest. She could trace the contours of his mouth, trace the slightly Roman nose, trace the slash of a jagged white scar above his left cheekbone. He was dressed casually: dark blue jeans, a white T-shirt with a grey cashmere sweater over the top to counter the chill of late autumn. She could smell the light lemon and lime notes of his aftershave—they swirled around her nostrils like a stupefying drug.

Frankie brought her gaze back to his and stepped back, her hands curled into fists in case she was tempted to touch him. Tempted to tell him she didn't care what strings he had in mind, she just wanted to be rescued from the shame of her father's crippling debts. But of course, her pride would never allow her to do something like that.

She flashed him an icy glare. 'I suppose you've come here to tell me you're the new owner.'

'I've bought the villa, yes. But I plan to give it to you.'

The words couldn't have been more shocking. Or pleasing. And it was this ambiguity of her feelings that was even more worrying. 'What do you mean?' Frankie was surprised her voice came out at all as her throat was so tight with a combination of hope and dread. Hope that she would be able to keep her home and dread that there would be a price to pay that had nothing to do with money.

He tapped the paperwork against the back of his other hand again. 'My lawyer has drawn up a contract. But I'm not going to discuss this out here in the foyer.' He nodded towards the library door. 'I think it's best if you're seated for this.'

Frankie widened her eyes but then quickly averted her gaze and stalked ahead of him to the library. No way was she going to let him see how much he unsettled her. She had spent years keeping men with nefarious motives at bay. Men who saw her, because of her social standing and her family wealth, as a trophy worth collecting. Even some of her girlfriends had only been friends with her because of her aristocratic background. It had made her distrustful of just about everyone but what choice did she have? She had been stung too many times in the past.

She was conscious of Gabriel following her, wondering if his satirical dark gaze was on the curves of her bottom. Was he comparing her to Miss Beach Baby?

Frankie turned around to face him once they were both inside the study. She folded her arms and planted her feet, giving him her best *make-me-sit-down-at-your-peril* glare. 'Tell me what's going on.'

His gaze flicked to the chair next to her. 'Sit.'

She straightened her shoulders like she was channelling a deportment guru. 'No, I will not sit. I'm a woman, not a dog.'

His gaze skated over her figure, leaving a trail of fiery heat in its wake. His eyes came back to hers and her heart went into arrhythmia again. The steely glint of determination in his eyes warned her she was seriously outmatched. 'I'm trying to help you, Francesca. It would be wise not to bite the hand that currently holds the deeds to your ancestral home.'

Frankie unfolded her arms and made fists of her hands. She wanted to slap that arrogantly assured expression off his face. Then she would punch him in his rock-hard stomach, even if it shattered every bone in her hand in the process. He was deliberately baiting her. Making her squirm like a bug on a corkboard. She had refused to date him in the past and now he wanted revenge with an indecent proposal. She plonked herself down in the chair and threw him a look that could have blistered the paint off every one of her ancestors' portraits. 'Do you think you can blackmail me to sleep with you?'

He was sitting on the corner of her father's desk, his long legs stretched out in front of him, casually crossed at the ankles. 'I prefer a less offensive term than blackmail, *cara.*'

She curled her lip. 'What term do you prefer to use? And for God's sake stop calling me *cara.*'

'The term I would use is charity.'

Frankie frowned so hard her forehead hurt. 'Charity?'

His lazy smile set that sail in her stomach flapping again. 'I am willing to gift you this house as well as the money to cover your father's debts if you'll agree to become my wife.'

Frankie shot out of her chair so fast it fell over with a thump. 'Your...*wife?*'

'Yes. My wife. But only for a year.'

Frankie opened and closed her mouth, unable to find her voice. For a shameful moment, unable to find a reason to refuse him when she thought of all that money. And her family home. Not to mention the hope of avoiding the public shame of millions of euros of debt.

No shame. No debt. No dirty little secrets let loose.

But she couldn't accept his proposal…could she? It was against everything she believed in. 'But I don't understand… Why would you only want to be married for a year?'

He got off the desk and came over and righted the chair she had knocked over, turning to face her again. 'You have something I need in the short term.'

Frankie swallowed, her legs suddenly feeling as if all her joints were only held together by pieces of string. She searched blindly for the desk behind her with her hands, gripping it to keep herself upright. His eyes were as dark as ebony, watchful, calculating, mesmerising. 'W-what?' It annoyed her to hear that crack in her voice. Annoyed and shamed her.

'Respectability.'

She rapid blinked. 'Respectability?' She gave a humourless laugh. 'Don't you realise the appalling mess my father left me in? There is absolutely nothing respectable about owing millions of—'

'No one needs to know anything about any of that if you marry me. I spoke to your father's lawyer on the phone just before you arrived. I will cover the entire debt on the condition that you marry me this weekend.'

Frankie's stomach dropped like an anchor. He was *serious* about this? He was prepared to marry her? To repay all that wretched money? 'This weekend? But it's Thursday now and—'

'You are aware of my family's reputation, *si*?' His mouth took on a twisted line.

'Yes, but everyone knows you're not—'

'Everyone but the board of directors I am currently trying to stay on,' Gabriel said. 'Your father was the one who nominated me last year but now he's gone, the other members are a little uneasy. But when I marry Marco's only daughter—an English/Italian aristocrat with an impeccable pedigree and reputation—it'll convince them I'm to be trusted.'

Frankie let go of her grip of the desk and clutched the neck of her silk blouse, worried her thumping heart was going to leap out and land on the carpet at Gabriel's feet. 'But I don't understand why you would choose me. I mean, we're not exactly friends. And you must know other aristocrats. Didn't you date a member of European royalty a few years ago?'

Gabriel came to stand in front of her, every inch of his six-foot-four frame exuding male power and potency. With him this close, she had to remind herself to breathe. She had to remind herself not to stare at his mouth, not to dream about it crushing hers. Had to remind herself she was a woman of pride and would not resort to marrying a man for his convenience.

But what about your convenience?

The voice of her conscience tapped her on the

shoulder like an unwelcome guest at a party. Gabriel's plan was tempting. Seriously, ridiculously tempting. One year of her life and she would be free of the shame of her father's gambling debts. She would have her family home back. It would remain in her possession. It would not be sold off to strangers or turned into a hotel or a grubby casino…

'I need your answer, Francesca. Yes or no.'

Frankie removed her hand from the neck of her blouse and scooted away from him, going behind her father's desk to keep a barrier between them. 'I need some time to think about this…' She disguised a gulping swallow, her thoughts in a messy fishing line tangle of fear.

Married for a year to Gabriel Salvetti? She had hoped to marry one day a man who loved her. Like her father had loved her mother. The mother she had never met since she'd died the day Frankie and her twin brother were born. Roberto had been stillborn and she had always wondered if she was responsible for both their deaths. Her father had never loved another woman since her mother's death. He had never remarried. He'd had the occasional relationship but no one had taken her mother's place.

That was the sort of love she wanted from a man.

Frankie gripped the back of her father's leather chair. 'What sort of marriage are you envisaging?' Her voice betrayed her with its faint note of trepidation.

His gaze flicked briefly to her mouth. 'That would be entirely up to you.'

She frowned, something in her stomach toppling from a high shelf. Something lower in her body flickering. Flaring. Flaming. 'What do you mean?'

'It can be a paper marriage or a normal one. Your choice.' His expression gave her no clue as to which one he wanted her to choose. A screen had come down over his face. And yet the atmosphere subtly changed as if an invisible third party had entered the room—mutual desire. It throbbed in the air like a current, back and forth between his gaze and hers. She felt it in her body, deep in her body—a flickering pulse that drew molten heat to her core.

Frankie sent the tip of her tongue out over her lips. 'And if I were to choose a paper one...would you get your...erm...needs met elsewhere?'

'No.'

His answer surprised her. He was a full-blooded man of thirty-two. He was in the prime of his life. He had a new lover every few weeks. He was always being photographed with a glamorous woman on his arm. 'You'd remain celibate for a whole year?' She couldn't keep the incredulity out of her voice.

'If you agree to a paper marriage, then that's the deal.' His eyes contained a hint of sardonic amusement. 'But of course, I would expect you, too, to remain celibate.'

Frankie wondered if he knew she was still a virgin. But how *could* he know? It wasn't something she brandished about. She was pretty sure her father hadn't known about her lack of a love life, especially since she'd been based in London the last four years, teaching in a special needs school. She had been unlucky with dating. A bad experience in her late teens had made her wary of dating men she didn't know. And the ones she knew, she didn't want to date. Like most young women her age, she dreamed of falling in love, but another part of her shied away from getting *that* close to someone.

To allow someone to see who she really was— the girl who had carried a curse since birth. Her birthday was her mother and brother's death day. If that wasn't a curse, she didn't know what was.

Frankie tightened her hold on the chair and fashioned her features into her trademark icy hauteur. 'I suppose you think if I agree to marry you, then I won't be able to help myself. That I'll beg you to make love to me or something.'

His mouth tilted in a smile so sexy the backs of her knees tingled. 'If so, I'd be happy to be of service.'

Frankie could feel her cheeks heating hot

enough to steam the wallpaper off the walls. 'I'm not in the habit of begging so don't hold your breath. But I still don't understand why you of all people would go to this amount of trouble and expense to rescue me from this situation.'

Gabriel picked up a paperweight off her father's desk and passed it from one hand to the other, his gaze focused on the trapped dandelion clock inside the glass sphere. She had given it to her father a couple of years ago because it reminded her of how she felt. Her fragile core of sensitivity shielded from the outside world. Gabriel held the sphere still for a moment, his thumb rolling over the top like he was caressing a woman's breast.

Her breast.

Frankie could actually feel her breast tingling. Damn the man for being so dangerously attractive. He could turn her on by remote. It was as if her body was tuned in to him. Tuned to his control and it was terrifying. Terrifying and yet…and yet…tempting.

He put the paperweight down again and met her gaze. 'Your father was a good man, Francesca. He took a chance on me early in my career. Like most people, he had his misgivings about me. But I made sure his one-off offer of help wasn't wasted.' He looked down to straighten the paperwork on the desk, glancing back at her to continue. 'Sure, he made a mess of things towards the end, but that was mostly due to his illness. I don't want his memory tainted or destroyed by what happened in the last few months of his life.'

Frankie had always been a little jealous of his relationship with her father. She hadn't been as close to her father as she would have liked but she mostly blamed herself. She was the one who had taken the love of his life away on the day she was born as well as his much longed for son and heir. It was hard to be close to someone who reminded you of what you had lost.

It was hard to be close to anyone when you carried such a horrible curse.

'But if you were so chummy with my father, then why didn't you come to his funeral?'

A flicker or something passed through his gaze. A flash of pain, a lightning strike of guilt. He pushed one of his hands through the ink-black thickness of his hair, his mouth set in a grim line. 'I was unable to get there due to circumstances beyond my control.'

Frankie folded her arms like a starchy schoolmistress. 'Did those circumstances involve a bikini-clad blonde bombshell?'

His eyebrows drew together in a frown. 'No. They did not.'

'Then what kept you away?'

The shutter came back down on his face. 'Suffice it to say it was a crisis and I was the only person who could deal with it at that time.'

She didn't know whether to believe him or not. She had been surprised, and yes, hurt not to see him at the funeral. He had only visited her father once in the last two months of his life and she hadn't been there at the time. She'd been out picking up more incontinence pads for her father and by the time she got back, the nurse on duty told her about Gabriel's brief visit. She wondered now if it had been deliberate. She hadn't realised how much she'd wanted to see him at the funeral until he didn't show. She couldn't explain why it had disappointed her so much other than she had felt completely overwhelmed with making all the arrangements on her own. And it was hard not to think it was her fault her mother and her twin brother Roberto hadn't been there to help her.

Frankie came out from behind the desk and went to stand in front of the windows that overlooked the parterre garden. She had spent most of her childhood playing in the gardens of the villa. It was her magical place, a place where she had exercised her imagination in order to make up for the absence of a mother and a sibling. She'd had a series of nannies and had never felt neglected in a physical sense. But emotionally she had felt isolated. Not necessarily unloved but not adored either.

She breathed out a long sigh and turned back to face Gabriel. 'Can I have a couple of days to think about this...proposal of yours?'

'I need your answer today. The press is sniffing around and I can't hold them off for ever.'

Panic beat a tattoo behind her ribcage. *Hurry. Stop. Hurry. Stop. Hurry. Stop.* She had never been good at decision-making under pressure. Her thoughts fired off in all directions like a box of accidentally lit fireworks. Marriage was a big step. A monumental step that should not be entered lightly—not according to her values. But what else could she do? Other people would suffer if that money was not paid back soon. Her father had borrowed money from friends and associates and it would only take one of them to sell their story to the press for her father's reputation to be permanently soiled.

But marrying Gabriel Salvetti?

Frankie covered her nose and mouth with her steepled hands, fighting to control her breathing. Everything was happening so fast. She didn't have time to think. To measure the risks. To escape. The room began to shift around her. The walls closing in, the furniture dark and looming and oppressive. She needed to sit down before she fell down. She reached for the chair but it was like searching through vaporous fog...

Suddenly a firm hand came down on her left

arm to steady her. 'Are you okay?' Gabriel's deep voice was full of concern. 'Breathe, *cara*.' He took both her hands and led her to the chair. 'Put your head down between your knees.' He guided her with a gentle hand pressed to the back of her head. 'That's it. Good girl.'

Frankie took several breaths, trying not to notice how nice it felt to have Gabriel's hand resting against her hair. A frisson of pleasure stole down from her scalp to her spine in a long streak of tickly warmth. He was standing so close to her she could feel the denim of his jeans through the silk sleeve of her top. And the potent heat of his muscled thigh. She couldn't remember a time when she had been so close to a man. Well, she could but it wasn't a time she wanted to recall in any detail.

But *this* was different.

Gabriel was different. He was respectful and caring in a way she had never expected him to be. His touch did strange things to her. Wicked things. Forbidden things. Unleashed thoughts and desires she couldn't suppress even though she wanted to. They were racing through her mind, triggering wanton images of him and her with entangled limbs and mouths pressed together in a passionate kiss, their bodies straining, yearning to get even closer.

Gabriel crouched down in front of her, his hand taking one of hers. 'Feeling better now?'

His espresso-black gaze meshed with hers, making her feel dizzy all over again. Dizzy with the need to feel his mouth on hers. She moistened her lips and watched as he followed the movement of her tongue. His eyes came back to hers and it was like a switch had been flicked.

The atmosphere tightened as if every stick of furniture in the room had taken a collective breath and held it. Held it. Held it...

Frankie glanced down at her pale hand encased in his. His fingers were dusted with dark masculine hair, the nails neat and square. She couldn't stop thinking about his hands on her body, touching her, pleasuring her. Awakening her. She tried to suppress a shiver but didn't quite manage it. 'I'm okay... I just felt a little faint...'

Gabriel released her hand and straightened, briefly resting a hand on her shoulder. 'I know my proposal must have come as a shock but I give you my word my motives are exactly as I've told you. There is no hidden agenda.'

Frankie couldn't hold his gaze. She didn't want him to see the naked need that was stirring in her body. A need she hadn't been aware of until now. She looked down at her hands resting on her thighs. 'Marriage seems a little extreme, though. I mean, what will we do after the year is up?'

'Get a divorce or an annulment.' He said it so casually as if it was as simple as ticking a box.

Frankie brought her gaze up to meet his. 'But you don't seem to be getting much out of the deal. You're prepared to spend millions for what? To be known as my husband?'

He moved to where she had been standing a few minutes before. His back turned to her as he too looked at the view outside. After a moment, he turned to face her but the light from outside put his face in shadow so she couldn't read his expression. 'You read the papers, do you not? You must have heard of my father's latest scandal?' The hardened tone of his voice alerted her to the shame he must feel about the criminal behaviour of his family. 'Drugs. The recent haul one of the biggest in the history of this country. Do you need me to go on?'

Frankie shook her head and bit her lip. 'No. It must be awful for you.'

'Damn right it's awful.' He moved to stand behind her father's desk, his hands gripping the back of the chair as she had done earlier. 'It's been virtually impossible to run my business lately. Deals have been cancelled at short notice. Big deals. Deals I worked on for months. Every time I turn up to a board meeting I can feel the tension, the uneasiness. Your situation is awful too, but we can fix both with a short-term marriage. It's not as if you're marrying a stranger. I will not treat you with anything but the utmost respect. You have my word on that.'

Put like that, it sounded a perfect plan. The trouble was the devil was in the detail. Devilish details such as her growing awareness of him. The physical awareness she could feel even now. The faint prickle of her breasts every time his gaze skated over her figure. The tingle in her lips when his eyes rested on her mouth. The hollow burning ache between her thighs when she thought about him touching her *there*. Frankie crossed her legs in an effort to quell the sensation but, if anything, it made it worse. It made her more aware of the secret tingling urgings of her body. 'But if we were to marry on paper, say, won't people expect us to be affectionate with each other, at least in public if not in private?'

His gaze drifted to her mouth for a brief moment. But then he blinked and brought his eyes back to hers, his expression an unreadable mask. 'We will have to touch on occasion but we can agree on what's appropriate.'

'You're making it sound so...so clinical,' Frankie said.

'The best solutions to tricky problems are formed without emotion clouding judgement.' He tapped his fingers on the back of the leather chair and added, 'Which brings me to the number one rule I insist on.'

'Rule?'

His eyes were as steady and determined as a marksman's. 'No falling in love with me.'

Frankie rocketed out of her chair as if it had burned her. 'Me fall in love with you?' She pointed her index finger at her chest and then at him. 'What about *you* falling in love with me?' This time she stabbed her index finger at him before pointing it back at herself. 'Works both ways, buddy.'

His jaw was set in an intractable line, his gaze suddenly cold and marble-hard. 'It's highly unlikely. No offence.'

Frankie gave a snort of laughter even though her ego was suffering a major crisis. A debilitating crisis. Was she so unlovable? Was every doubt she had about herself true? 'Let me tell you what I find offensive. You thinking I would be so desperate as to accept your stupid proposal.'

Gabriel put his hand on the paperwork he'd placed on the desk earlier and pushed it across so she could see it. 'The villa will be placed back in your name as soon as we're married. It's written in this contract. We will go on a short honeymoon to the south of France for the sake of appearances.'

A honeymoon? Frankie's gaze went to the contract even though she hated herself for it. She didn't want to need Gabriel's help but who else would or could help her? Some of the people she had thought of asking had already lent her father money and were impatient to be repaid. And who else had *that* sort of money?

She read through the contract, wondering yet

again why he was going to so much trouble to help her. But then she recalled what he'd said about his father's latest scandal and the board position Gabriel was trying to keep. Success was important to men like Gabriel. He thrived on it. It was why her rejection of him had nettled him.

He didn't give up on a goal.

He found ways, *made* ways, to achieve it.

Frankie pushed the contract back to his side of the desk. 'It seems to me you're paying a very high price for respectability, marrying a woman you swear you could never love.'

'It's best if we both keep our emotions out of this, Francesca.' He softened it with a small on-off smile that didn't reach his eyes. 'And if we were to consummate the marriage, I absolutely insist on the use of contraception. No exceptions. Understood?'

Frankie held her hand up. 'Whoa there. Aren't you jumping ahead of yourself? I haven't agreed to marry you yet and I—'

'You will marry me, *cara*. You have too much at stake not to.'

Frankie wished it wasn't true. But the thought of losing her home for the sake of her stubborn pride was an ask too big, an even bigger ask than marrying a man who claimed he would never fall in love with her. Was there any crueller blow to a feminine ego than *that* insulting declaration?

Frankie blew out a breath of resignation, keeping her gaze out of reach of his. 'It looks like I've got no choice…'

He came from behind the desk and stood next to her. 'Look at me, Francesca.'

She brought her gaze up to his dark inscrutable one. He searched her gaze for a long moment, then he lifted his hand to her face and gently traced the curve of her cheek from just below her ear to the base of her chin. Every nerve in her face tingled at his touch, her heart skipping a beat, her breath coming to a screeching halt.

His mouth slanted in a knowing smile. 'I'm helping you. You're helping me. That's all this is. Do I make myself clear?'

Frankie pulled out of his hold and pointedly rubbed at her chin. 'I have some rules too. You don't get to touch me unless I say so.'

'Sounds reasonable, although there will be occasions when we're in public that my asking permission will look odd, *si*?'

'Okay, but I mostly meant when we're alone.' Frankie elevated her chin to a defiant height. 'And it's going to be a paper marriage.'

A glint appeared in his gaze as if the wick of an irresistible challenge had been lit. 'Are you absolutely sure about that, *cara mia*?'

CHAPTER TWO

GABRIEL HELD FRANKIE'S defiant grey-blue gaze. He could see the battle playing out over her beautiful features. She reminded him of a haughty princess who had suffered an insult from a lowly stable-hand. She wanted to slap him but her classy up-bringing prevented her from doing so. Her small fists kept clenching and unclenching, her shoulders stiff with bottled-up emotion. It was one of the things he found so cute about her. The way she was so buttoned up like she had stepped straight out of the Regency period.

'I told you not to call me that.' Her eyes flashed like lightning and his groin tightened at the thought of seeing those unusual eyes shining with lust instead of loathing. Grey one minute, blue the next, her eyes reminded him of the lake outside with its shifting blue moods and smoky grey shadows.

'People will expect me to speak to you affectionately once we're married,' he said, privately smiling at her tightly compressed mouth. The mouth he couldn't stop thinking about kissing. Lush, full lips shaped like a perfect cupid's bow. A mouth built for passion, for pleasure. A mouth he craved to taste, to explore, to tease and tantalise.

She thought him beneath her—understandable given his criminal family—but while four years ago she had rebuffed his offer of a date, now she was the one who couldn't say no.

He liked proving people wrong. It filled an emptiness inside him. He had spent most of his life trying to avoid comparisons with his father and it satisfied him to prove he was nothing like anyone in his family.

Gabriel was a self-made man who lived by his own moral code, not by the warped and corrupt one of his family. Marrying Francesca Mancini was his way of honouring her father. Marco Mancini had put aside his prejudice about his upbringing and had given him a chance. A chance Gabriel had not wasted. Marco's timely advice and direction had meant Gabriel had been able to expand his career, buying and selling property, and in the process had amassed huge amounts of his own wealth. Last year, Marco had invited him to an exclusive board of company directors. The networking alone was worth gazillions. He would never forget the risk Marco had been prepared to take on a young man from a notoriously disreputable family.

The decision to marry Frankie was a calculated move on Gabriel's part. Calculated because he was not going to stand by and watch her father's good name be sullied by an unfortunate set of circumstances during the last months of Marco Mancini's life.

But there was more to his offer than a simple favour to a dead man.

Gabriel wanted Frankie. He'd wanted her ever since she had rejected him, because deep down, he knew she wanted him too, but she refused to acknowledge it. She was a challenge he couldn't resist. He wasn't an egotist. He was a man who set goals and did all he could possibly do, within reason and moral boundaries, to achieve them.

Even if—and it was a big if—she didn't want their marriage to be consummated, once he had his ring on her finger he would have won.

Getting her to marry him would be a victory in itself.

Frankie spun away from him, her wildly curly dark brown hair pulled back into a ponytail swinging from side to side as if even her hair was annoyed with him. She had her English aristocrat mother's colouring—creamy white skin and those beautiful eyes with their fringe of thick lashes and black eyebrows. She had curves in all the right places, curves he longed to explore in real time instead of dream time.

'I'm afraid there isn't time for a church wedding,' Gabriel said.

She turned to face him, her expression so icy he could have shivered. 'If you think I would stand in front of a priest and make promises I have no intention of keeping, then you'd better think again.'

'People will understand given it's only been a few weeks since your father's death.' He paused for a beat before adding, 'I can only imagine how much you miss him.'

Something flickered through her gaze like a zephyr across the surface of a lake. But then she shifted her gaze and straightened one of the books on the shelves nearby. 'Sometimes I find it hard to accept he's no longer here…' She glanced at him again. 'When I came in just before and heard you in here, I thought it was him. That he wasn't dead and this horrible nightmare of his squandered wealth was just a bad dream.' Her mouth twisted. 'If only, huh?'

Gabriel was no stranger to grief. His mother had died when he was nine and it had taken him years to stop missing her. For a decade he'd secretly kept one of her jumpers so he could still smell her. The fallout from her death had not just affected him but his two younger brothers Ricci and Lorenzo and most especially his baby sister Carli, who had only been two years old.

Gabriel had tried to fill in the gaps, to be a parent figure, but his younger brothers idolised their father and nothing Gabriel did or said could influence them. He'd had more of a chance with Carli. As a small child, she had hero-worshipped him and was mostly frightened of their father and his violent outbursts, not to mention the shady characters who came and went from the house. Gabriel hoped and prayed he *still* had a chance with his little sister, but Carli had been struggling on and off with an eating disorder since her teens.

Even now, when Gabriel saw a family group with two parents and small children, smiling, loving, belonging, razorblades would twist and churn in his gut. He hadn't yet saved his baby sister from her inner demons but he wasn't giving up. Not yet. Not ever.

Gabriel came to stand in front of her near the bookshelves. 'He was a good man, Francesca. One of the best. And he loved you and only wanted what was best for you.'

The fleeting shadow was back in her gaze, making them appear more grey than blue, like troubled clouds. 'I suppose compared to your father, mine must have seemed Father of the Year material.'

You don't know the half of it. Gabriel kept his expression blank. He had taught himself not to reveal too much of how he felt about his father. The term 'father' was too nice a term to use in reference to the man who had sired him and his siblings. 'There is no comparison.' He glanced at his watch in an effort to change the subject. 'It's time for a drink to celebrate our upcoming marriage, which reminds me…' He fished in his pocket and took out the engagement ring he'd bought for her. He took her left hand and slipped the diamond cluster over her ring finger.

Frankie glanced up at him and then back at the ring, her small white teeth chewing at her lower lip. 'It's beautiful…but it looks ridiculously expensive. I mean, you've already spent so much money and—'

He held her hand in both of his, squeezing it gently. 'Stop worrying about money. We're helping each other, remember?'

Her shimmering eyes met his and something moved in his chest, like a small creature scrabbling through one of the chambers of his heart. He released her hand and stepped back, trying to ignore the tingle in his fingers. Trying to ignore the urge to kiss her. 'What were your plans this evening?' He was proud of the neutral tone of his voice.

'I was just going to go back to my hotel and have dinner.'

'Why have you been staying in a hotel?' Gabriel asked. 'I was surprised when the agent told me you hadn't been here since the funeral.'

'I thought it would be easier to keep away

while the real estate agent showed potential buyers through.' She fiddled with the ring on her finger, avoiding his gaze. 'And since Papa died here… it felt too empty and lonely… I had to lay off the staff to keep the running costs down.'

'Would you consider staying here if I stayed with you?'

Indecision flicked through her gaze. 'Is that wise?'

Probably not. But he would get his self-control in hand. 'We will be married in a matter of forty-eight hours. People will expect us to live together.'

Frankie slipped out of his hold and hugged her arms around her middle. She suddenly looked much younger than her twenty-five years. Young and vulnerable. It was rare for her to show vulnerability and he had yet to see her shed tears. Her default position was anger—or at least in her dealings with him. He didn't know too much about her dealings with other men. She somehow kept her private life private—rare for someone of her social standing. But that was another reason she was perfect wife material—no salacious scandals in her past.

'You'll be safe with me, Francesca. I will honour your decision to keep our relationship platonic.' It nearly killed him to make that promise but he would see it through if she didn't change her mind. He was not the sort of man to cajole or manipulate a woman into having sex. He didn't need to.

'Thank you.' If she was relieved by his promise, she didn't show it. Her beautiful face was as still as frost on a lawn but behind her grey-blue eyes he sensed a storm was brewing.

Within an hour, Gabriel had organised Frankie's things to be packed and sent over from her hotel back to Villa Mancini. And now they were seated at an exclusive restaurant a short drive from the villa overlooking Lake Como, the third largest lake in Italy. The mountains beyond rose majestically, creating a stunning backdrop to the deep waters of the lake. Frankie never tired of looking at the view and even though she had been based in London for the last four years, she considered the lake and its surrounds as one of the most beautiful places in the world.

And it was the place where for a brief space of time she had been held her in her mother's arms. Of course, she had no conscious memory of her mother, but sometimes she wondered if her infant brain had registered the loss of her mother and twin brother. Wouldn't that explain the terrible emptiness she felt when she saw mothers with their infant children?

Frankie was so caught up in her thoughts she hadn't noticed Gabriel's steady gaze. 'Sorry, I was miles away.' She picked up her glass with the top shelf French champagne he had selected and took a sip. 'Mmm, lovely. You have good taste.'

'For a man from the wrong side of the tracks?' His tone was wry, so too the twist to his mouth.

Frankie put her glass back down. 'I didn't mean it like that. I just meant—'

'It's fine, *cara*.' He moved the base of the glass in a small and precise quarter turn like he was unlocking the code to a safe.

'Do you ever see him? Your father, I mean?'

'No.' The word was as final as a full stop.

'When was the last time you saw—'

'Leave it, Francesca.' His expression had turned to stone. Cold. Hard. Impenetrable stone.

'Why do you always call me Francesca?'

His eyes met hers across the table and something unfurled in her stomach. 'It's a beautiful name. Regal. Sophisticated.' His voice lowered a notch, the hint of huskiness making the base of her spine fizz.

'Is that how you see me?' She could have bitten off her tongue for fishing for compliments but couldn't seem to help herself.

He picked up his glass but she got the feeling he had only done it to do something with his hands for he didn't raise it to his lips. 'I'm not sure you'd want to hear how I see you.'

'Try me. Go on. Tell me.' Seriously, she should

not drink champagne. It loosened her tongue way too much. It made her daring and flirtatious and the one thing she never did was flirt. Never.

His smile was crooked and so damn sexy she could feel her lower body tingling. 'You're a passionate woman underneath that ice princess thing you have going on.' The husky note was back in his voice and his gaze lingered on her mouth as if he were thinking of how it would respond to his own.

Frankie's cheeks could have scorched the top of a *crème brûlée*. 'You don't know anything about me. You just think you do.'

He gave a soft laugh and tipped his head back to take a sip of his champagne. He put the glass back on the table, watching her with an amused gaze. 'You're ashamed of how you're attracted to me. Nice girls like you don't do bad boys like me.'

Frankie was having trouble staying seated. Her lower body was betraying her with hot little flickers of unbidden desire. Desire she didn't want to feel. Not for him. She wasn't so much ashamed of her attraction towards him. She was frightened. It was too powerful, too intense, too out of control for her to handle. She picked up her glass again, her posture cool and composed, but inside she was trembling with need. Could he see it? Could he sense it? He seemed to have an uncanny ability to see through the cool mask she wore. 'I wouldn't have thought a worldly man like you would be interested in a nice girl. She would be too boring and pedestrian for your taste, would she not?'

'That depends.'

'On what?'

His dark lustrous eyes pulsed with a message as old as time—hot, raw, earthy male desire. 'On which nice girl you're talking about.'

Frankie chest fluttered like there was a frantic robin trapped in her ribcage. This conversation was getting into dangerous territory. She didn't flirt with men. Not any more. She had flirted once in the past and a relationship developed out of it, only for her to find out the man had only wanted to date her because of her family wealth and status. He'd been a trophy collector intent on sleeping with her so he could boast about it to his friends. Thankfully she had ended the relationship before the deed was done, although the horrible names he called her made her feel just as sullied.

But flirting with Gabriel felt *different*.

Dangerous, yes, but not because she was afraid of him. She was afraid of herself. Of how she might betray herself by responding to him like a wanton nymph.

Frankie looked at him over the rim of her crystal champagne flute. 'Why don't you want to have children?' She hadn't realised she was going to ask the question until it was out of her mouth. But if Gabriel found the abrupt subject change off-putting he gave no indication.

'I don't feel the need to pass on my genes.'

'Because of your family?'

His dark gaze had Keep Out written all over it. 'What about you? Do you want children one day?' His tone was casual. Almost too casual, as if he was uncomfortable making polite conversation on the subject of kids but was determined not to show it. And he was convincing…except she sensed a wariness in him. It was there in the stillness of his features. A stillness that seemed to involve every muscle in his face, every muscle in his body. Every eyelash fringing those bottomless brown eyes.

Frankie began to toy with the stem of her glass, her gaze moving out of reach of his to watch the play of her fingers. 'I don't know… I figure I've got a bit of time before I have to make up my mind.' She placed her hand back in her lap and looked at him again. 'I'm not sure what sort of mother I'd be. I mean, I grew up without one. It's not as if I've had a role model, other than nannies and babysitters. And they were *paid* to look after me. It's not the same thing, is it?'

Behind the screen of his gaze something shifted. A flicker. A shadow. A ghost. 'No. I imagine not.'

A silence passed.

'What's your mother like?' Frankie asked. 'Is she still married to your father?'

'She's dead.' The words were like bullets. Bang. Bang. Gabriel drank from his glass and placed it back on the table with another thud of *subject closed* finality.

'I'm sorry. What happened?'

He drew in a savage-sounding breath, his gaze hard and black as onyx. 'One thing you need to learn about me, Francesca. I don't like discussing my family. Do I make myself clear?'

'Perfectly clear.' Frankie sat back in her chair and surveyed him for a long moment. His eyes had that impenetrable screen back in place. His jaw was set like concrete, the strong tendons in the backs of his hands taut and ropy with tension. Now that she had experienced the shame of her father's fall from grace, she could only imagine how awful it must be for Gabriel to live with the ongoing shame of his criminal family. Several members of his extended family were currently in jail and his father was awaiting trial for a string of new drug offences.

It was strange but in spite of Gabriel's background, she had never felt he was a bad man. She had been put off by his arrogance when he'd asked her out four years ago. Put off by his assumption that she wouldn't be able to resist his charm. And it had been a close call if she were to be strictly honest with herself. She had been tempted.

She was *still* tempted.

After a stretched silence, Gabriel released a long sigh. 'I'm sorry. It's just I've spent most of my adult life *not* thinking about my family.'

Frankie reached for his hand and placed hers on top of it. 'I'm sorry for pushing you to talk about something that's so obviously painful. I'll try not to do it again.'

He turned her hand over and encased her fingers in the warm tensile strength of his. A half-smile softened his features and something jerked in her chest as if a miniature pony had kicked against her heart. She looked down at their joined hands and heat spilled and simmered between her legs. His touch did strange things to her body. It made her think of being possessed by him, moving with him in the throes of scorching hot passion.

A passion she had never experienced.

Their food arrived at that point and during dinner the conversation drifted onto neutral ground. Frankie was surprised she was actually enjoying herself. The food was amazing and Gabriel seemed to be trying to entertain her with amusing anecdotes about his work as a property developer. But after a while, she couldn't help noticing the interested glances of the other diners. One woman took her phone out and aimed it their way to take a picture. Frankie lowered her head and turned to face the window rather than be captured. 'Don't look now but someone is taking our photo,' she said in an undertone.

'Better get used to it, *cara*.' His tone was brimful of world-weary resignation. 'I can't go anywhere at the moment without the press following. But it will hopefully die down once we're married.'

Married. The word made her feel things she shouldn't be feeling. It was supposed to be a paper marriage. That was what she'd told him. That was what she'd insisted on.

But when he helped her out of her chair a short time later, his touch triggered sensations in her body she couldn't control. The strong band of his arm encircled her waist as he led her out of the restaurant and a wave of longing coursed through her. Even if she had been wearing skyscraper heels, he towered over her, making her feel feminine in a way she had never felt before.

They came to his car and his hand moved from her waist to rest on her hip as he opened the passenger door for her. She slipped into the car and took the seatbelt he'd pulled down for her. His fingers setting off spot fires when they touched hers.

How could getting into a car be so damn sexy? It was ridiculous.

She was ridiculous.

Frankie glanced at him once he was behind the wheel. Would she ever get tired of looking at him? He was like a fallen angel. Handsome as sin with a raw masculinity than made her blood fizz and simmer in her veins. Her gaze drifted to his powerful thighs as he worked the gears, the throaty roar of the engine under his command like a panther on the prowl.

Gabriel met her gaze and winked at her. 'Don't worry. I'll keep you safe.'

What if she didn't want to be safe?

CHAPTER THREE

GABRIEL CONCENTRATED ON driving back to the villa but he was conscious of the throb of sensual energy in the car. He had caught the tail end of a couple of Frankie's covert glances and wondered if she was thinking what he was thinking. If she was feeling what he was feeling. The hot rush of desire that refused to die down. The blistering burn of need. He would not make a move on her. He wanted her to own her desire for him. He saw it in her eyes. He felt it in her touch.

He could damn near taste it in the air.

He gripped the steering wheel tighter to stop himself reaching across to touch her slim and shapely thigh. 'Will you be able to take a year off work?' He was surprised at how even his tone was, so casual, so bland when his body was boiling with hot-blooded lust.

She shifted in her seat and he felt rather than saw her gaze. 'You're expecting me to give up work? Isn't that a little outdated of you?'

Gabriel shrugged one shoulder. 'I have no problem with you working but not if you're working in another country from me. I'm not into long-distance relationships.'

'But our relationship is on paper so why would it matter?'

'I'm not having everyone commenting on the fact my wife is unable to bear living under the same roof as me, that's why.'

'Why don't you move to London instead?' Frankie asked. 'You have plenty of business there, don't you?'

'I have an apartment there, yes, but my home is in Milan. It's where I spent most of my time, other than when I travel for work.' He sent her a quick glance. 'I'm the one putting myself out for you, remember. The least you could do is move to Italy for the year. It's not as if you won't be adequately compensated for the inconvenience.'

The silence was palpable.

Was he asking too much of her? He didn't want distance between them, paper marriage or not. He needed a year of her time. It would take that long for the board of directors to build their trust in him.

Gabriel let out a rough sigh. 'I'm not trying to be difficult.'

'Seems like it to me.' She folded her arms across her middle. 'You expect me to uproot my life and fall into your plans like some obedient little wife from the nineteenth century who has nothing better to do than embroider doilies all day. I've already taken two months of leave when I looked after my father.'

'I'm afraid this is not negotiable. I want you by my side otherwise no one will believe this is a genuine relationship.'

'And if I say no?'

'The deal is off.'

He saw her look at her engagement ring. She even touched it as if in two minds whether to rip it off and throw it at him. But then she let out a defeated sigh. 'Do you ever lose an argument?'

'Not any more.'

When they got back to the villa, Gabriel excused himself to see to some emails and Frankie went to her room where he had taken her bag earlier that evening. It felt strange to be back home. She hadn't spent a night under this roof since her father's death. But the villa felt like an entirely different place with Gabriel's presence.

It had been pointless arguing with him about her maintaining her life in London. A part of her understood where he was coming from. Her job, as much as she enjoyed it, was hardly on the same scale as his. But she didn't want to fall too easily into his plans as if she had no mind or will or aspirations of her own. One of the reasons she wanted to keep her family home was a vision she harboured about using part of it as a holiday retreat for disadvantaged kids. Many of the children she taught came from difficult backgrounds. Some of them had never even been on a holiday. It was such a stark contrast from her privileged upbringing where exotic holidays were the norm.

In some ways, Frankie thought her father had taken her on expensive holidays with the current nanny in tow because he hadn't wanted to be left alone with her. Even when she was a teenager he insisted on her bringing one or two of her friends. But it had become difficult for her to work out who were her genuine friends and who were freeloaders who couldn't wait to be taken to St Barts or Aspen or wherever.

Once she'd unpacked, Frankie went to one of the larger spare bedrooms to prepare it for Gabriel. She hesitated outside the master bedroom. It hadn't been slept in for twenty-five years. Her father had been unable to sleep in there after her mother's death. It had been years before he'd asked one of the housekeepers to remove his wife's things. Frankie remembered the day, remembered too the slump of depression her father slipped into that seemed to go on for months. In the end, she was glad she had to go back to her convent boarding school in England.

Frankie moved on past down the hall to another

suite overlooking the lake. It was further away from her room and until she got her self-control into gear, that could only be a good thing.

When she came downstairs a short time later, Gabriel came out of the library.

'I've made a room up for you,' she said. 'It's the fourth on the right.'

'Thank you. But I could have made up my own bed. You don't have to wait on me. Do you want the same housekeeper and ground staff as before or will I engage new ones?'

Frankie's stomach plummeted at the thought of paying staff wages. But the villa was way too big for her to handle even if she had loads of spare time on her hands. 'My father's previous housekeeper retired upon his death. If we could keep it to a skeleton staff…say one housekeeper and two gardeners?'

'I don't expect you to pay for the staff. I'll see to that.'

Had he read her mind? Disturbing thought. What else would he see in there? She could feel her cheeks warming up and shifted her gaze. 'Thank you. It's very generous of you.' Her teeth worried her lower lip before she added, 'I don't know how I'll ever be able to repay you.'

'Stay married to me for a year. That's all I want.'

Frankie found it hard to hold his gaze. She was worried she would betray herself by staring at his mouth. But it was impossible not to glance at it. Impossible not to ache to feel those firm masculine lips against her own.

He came towards her, standing within touching distance but keeping his hands by his sides. 'There will be legal work to see to tomorrow. I've organised my lawyer to meet us here. After that you can shop for a wedding dress unless you happen to have one on stand-by in your wardrobe?' Was that a hint of mockery in his dark as night gaze? Did he think she was a hope chest girl? Desperately squirrelling away things for her trousseau, ready for the day when a man finally swept her off her feet?

Frankie lifted her chin and narrowed her gaze. 'You want me to wear a proper wedding dress? Really? Even though it's not a church wedding?'

'I'm giving you the option to be a traditional bride. Take it or leave it.' His voice was calm but there was a flicker of tension in his jaw.

'And where will this wedding ceremony be conducted?' Frankie didn't hold back on the ice in her tone.

'The celebrant could do it here in the garden, unless you have somewhere else you'd prefer?'

Frankie felt a little ambushed by his suggestion. As a young girl she had often dreamed of being married in the garden of the villa. It had been part of her imaginative play to imagine herself walking up the wisteria walk on her father's arm towards her dashingly handsome, madly-in-love-with-her groom.

But her father was dead and this wasn't a love marriage.

Frankie bit down on her lip. 'I do have a wedding dress... It was my mother's. My father kept it for me. I think I know where it is in the attic. But I'm not sure what condition it's in. It may need dry-cleaning or at least airing.'

'We have a couple of days to see to that.' Gabriel took her left hand and rubbed the pad of his thumb over her diamond ring. 'Is there anyone you'd like to invite? Relatives from England? Close friends?'

Frankie sighed and looked at their joined hands. 'I hardly know my English relatives. They mostly drifted out of my life after my mother and twin brother died.'

'I didn't know you had a twin.' His shocked tone brought her gaze back up. 'Your father never said anything to me about a sibling.'

Frankie slipped her hand out of his before she got addicted to his touch. 'Yes, well, he didn't like to talk about Mama's passing, much less talk about Roberto's stillbirth. Of course, it would've been a terribly traumatic time for him, looking forward to the much-anticipated birth of twins, only to lose his firstborn son and then his wife to a massive post-partum haemorrhage.'

'A terrible, unthinkable tragedy.' His tone was deep with gravitas, his expression deeply furrowed.

'One of the nannies let slip that I'd been a twin when I was about four or five. There were no photos of Roberto. I don't suppose with the shock of Mama's death anyone thought to take any. I only have a few of myself as an infant that one of the nannies took.'

'I know your father was reluctant to speak of your mother. But once after a few drinks, he showed me a photo of her. You're very like her. I got the sense it made him depressed to talk about her. Understandable given the tragic circumstances. But I often wondered why he didn't marry again. He was certainly young enough to have more children if he'd wanted them.'

'He had occasional short and discreet relationships,' Frankie said. 'But I got the feeling the women he dated couldn't handle competing with a ghost. He still had all Mama's clothes still in the wardrobe up until a couple of years ago. I found it a bit creepy to be perfectly honest.'

A shadow passed over his face. 'It must have been very difficult for you growing up without a mother.'

'Yes, well, what you never have, you never miss—or so they say, whoever "they" are.' She released another sigh and frowned. 'But I do miss her. I miss the idea of her. I miss the concept of a who and what a mother is. It's like I have this great big empty echoing vacuum inside here.' She made a fist of her hand and bumped it against her chest. 'Nothing can fill it. I don't have the first idea how to.' Frankie lowered her hand and her gaze, suddenly embarrassed and ashamed she'd let her guard down. What was she doing spilling her guts to him? What was she hoping for? Sympathy? Understanding? A big warm comforting hug?

Gabriel took her hand again, his fingers warm and soothing around hers. 'The loss of a mother so young must surely be felt on some level, even if it's not a conscious one.'

Frankie looked into his eyes and wondered if he was thinking of the loss of his own mother. He hadn't told her anything about her. He had refused to speak about any of his family. Were those flickers and shadows in his gaze the hoofmarks of his loss?

Were they the silent footsteps of his grief?

'Gabriel…how old were you when you lost your mother?'

At first, she wondered if he was even going to answer. He released her hand and stepped back from her, his expression so still it was as if he was mentally locking away his memories. His emotions. His pain. And of course, there would be pain. He could ignore or deny its existence but she could sense it in him. It was there in the shadows of his chocolate brown eyes. It was in the stoic strength and steely set of his jaw.

'I was nine.' His tone was flat. Emotionless. He could have been describing the death of a house plant.

'Do you remember her?' She knew it was a push too far but she asked it anyway.

'We have a big day ahead of us tomorrow,' he said in the same toneless voice. 'I'll let you get to bed. Goodnight.'

Frankie stood and watched as he turned and went back into the library, the door closing behind him. He was the most perplexing, enigmatic man. So much of him was closed off. Locked away. His thoughts and feelings a secret code she didn't have the password for.

Would she ever?

CHAPTER FOUR

GABRIEL WAITED UNTIL he was sure Frankie had gone to bed before he went upstairs to his room. Not that he expected to sleep. He was shocked to hear about her twin brother. It was hard not to feel deeply sad that she and her father had been blighted by such terrible heart-breaking tragedy. But he couldn't help feeling a little stung her father hadn't shared Roberto's stillbirth with him. But their relationship had been an unusual one. He had enjoyed the older man's company and admired and respected him, but he had realised early on that not many people got truly close to Marco Mancini. But then, wasn't *he* the same? They had been kindred spirits in human isolation. Had it been too painful for Marco to speak of the loss of his baby son? Had it been too raw to even mention in passing?

Gabriel hated talking about his own pain. His own shame. The shame that stuck to him like thick putrid-smelling mud. He had told Marco very little of his own upbringing. Virtually no one knew about the early days before wealth came bounding in the Salvetti door. Wealth Gabriel had welcomed and never questioned. He had mentioned nothing to Marco about the hunger of his early childhood, the beatings, the desperate attempts to keep his siblings safe from sleazy predators. The feast and famine rollercoaster when yet another get-rich-quick scheme of his father's went well or turned sour. In those early years Gabriel had begged on the streets in order to provide food for his younger siblings. He had stolen fruit from people's gardens, had snatched up diners' leftovers in street cafés.

And then everything changed. It was like a miracle and Gabriel had never questioned it because it was such a relief not to have to struggle any more. To not feel burning aching hunger ripping and clawing at his guts. To not feel burning aching shame. He had enjoyed the bounty—the move to a better house, a classy suburb instead of a slum. The housekeeping staff: the cooks and cleaners, the gardeners, the butlers, the chauffeurs.

The status.

The security.

The safety.

He had taken advantage of the private education his father had offered him and his siblings. He had enjoyed it all until the day he turned eighteen when he'd found out the truth about his father's wealth.

The filthy truth that made Gabriel feel ashamed of every euro that had been spent on him. Every dirty blood-and-pain-and-drug-stained euro.

He had been educated, dressed and fed on the proceeds of drugs. The drugs that poisoned people, destroyed lives. The same drugs that had killed his mother, given to her by his father to stop her going to the police about his nefarious dealings. For all the years before that Gabriel had been told his mother had killed herself. Gabriel knew deep in his DNA there was no way his mother would have chosen to end her life, leaving four young children behind. At eighteen, once the ugly truth was out, he walked away from his father, begging his siblings to come with him, to remove themselves from the stain of the family name, but his brothers had refused out of a perverse type of loyalty to their father. They had loved the money and status more than morality.

And Carli had been so desperate to belong to a family it had taken her most of her teenage years to recognise their father for what he was—a criminal stand-over man who got rid of people if they got on the wrong side of him. And even now that she did acknowledge their father's criminal activity, Carli was still not always keen on Gabriel's help.

But Frankie's father must have sensed some strange fellowship of suffering with Gabriel for the way he gave him that chance all those years ago. And for that he would be grateful for ever. Although he still felt annoyed with himself for not realising the financial mess Marco had got himself into until it was almost too late. But he was putting it right now and in a couple of days Frankie would be his wife.

Gabriel had met Frankie in passing a couple of times in her teens when she was home from her convent boarding school in England, the same school where her mother and grandmother had been educated. She had pretended not to notice him on those occasions but her blushes and covert glances had given her away. He could still remember the first time he shook her hand on meeting her when she was seventeen. It had sent a fizzing sensation straight to his groin. At twenty-three back then, he'd been no hormonally driven teenager— he'd had several lovers by then and was shocked that a slip of a girl could do that to him. Could have that stun-gun effect on him.

And she still did.

Frankie didn't go straight to bed even though she was feeling the exhaustion of the day catching up with her like a stalking predator. But she couldn't rest until she found her mother's wedding dress. She needed to know if it was suitable to wear or whether she needed to buy a new one. But when she located the dress in a chest in the attic, she knew that no other dress would do. She peeled back the layers of protective tissue paper covering the dress and held it against her body. The exquisite Chantilly lace and satin dress fell in soft folds to the floor around her ankles. It could have been made specifically for her.

The pearly white of the dress complemented her colouring and the shape and fit of the bodice and skirt showcased her feminine curves. There was a hand-embroidered lace veil and a princess tiara to attach it to. She couldn't imagine wearing any other dress but this, but was it the right thing to do? Her mother had married her father in a genuine love match. Would Frankie be desecrating this beautiful dress by wearing it to marry a man she didn't love and who didn't love her? A man who had insisted no feelings, no emotions, no sentiment be involved in their arrangement?

Frankie took the dress back to her bedroom and hung it on a satin-covered coat hanger in the walk-in wardrobe. She smoothed the lace skirt and wondered what emotions her mother had felt on the day of her wedding. Had she been excited? Nervous?

She sighed and stepped back from the dress and all it represented. She had to stick to the plan. Marrying Gabriel was the only way out of the financial mess her father had left and she would do it and do it as coldly and clinically as Gabriel.

No feelings. No emotions. No regrets.

* * *

Frankie joined Gabriel and his lawyer in the library the following morning after breakfast. Gabriel had given her the paperwork to read over beforehand and she was not surprised to see he had organised a pre-nuptial agreement. She had no issue with it—it was a reasonable thing to do under the circumstances, but it was yet another jarring reminder of how different their marriage was going to be. How different their relationship was—neither friends nor foes but something in the murky grey area between.

Frankie signed where she was asked to sign and watched Gabriel write his own distinctive signature on the documents. *Sheesh*. Even the way he held the pen in his hand made her think of sex. She imagined those clever capable fingers stroking her, touching her in places no one had ever touched her before. She suppressed a shudder, wondering how much he had told his lawyer about their relationship. If the older man seemed surprised by the details he had drawn up for his client, he was too professional to show it. He left a short time later expressing his best wishes for their wedding day.

Gabriel closed the door on the lawyer's exit and turned to Frankie. 'I hope that wasn't too painful for you?'

Frankie flicked a wayward curl away from her face. 'Why would it be? I have no problem with you protecting your wealth.' She went to turn away but he stalled her by touching her lightly on the arm. Even through the sleeve of her top his touch made her tingle with awareness.

His hand dropped back by his side as if he didn't dare to touch her for too long. Did he feel it too? The zap of electricity each time they touched? Was that why his gaze darkened when it met hers? 'In spite of what anyone else thinks, this marriage is only for a year. I'm not prepared to jeopardise my assets for a relationship that isn't going to last.'

Frankie lifted her chin. 'Do you have a strict time limit on all of your relationships?'

'Only when necessary.'

Did he really think *she* would be the one who wouldn't want their marriage to end? That *she* would be the one begging him to continue their relationship indefinitely? 'Oh, so you think it's necessary to keep reminding me this set-up of ours has a use-by date?' Frankie threw him a frosty glare. 'I got the memo, Gabriel. You don't have to keep hammering it home.'

He held her glare so easily she might as well have been smiling meekly at him. 'By the way, only my lawyer and us need to know this is what it is.' His voice contained a steely thread of implacability. 'My household staff will assume it's a love match. I expect you to tell your friends and acquaintances the same. That's what I'm telling the press when I release a statement after we are married.'

Frankie tried not to think of how many people would see the news of their marriage in the press. Hundreds. Millions. Multiple millions. Possibly billions. She would be living a lie and yet what other choice did she have? It was either that or let everyone know what her father had been up to in the last few months of his life. And for her to declare bankruptcy. 'Then how will you explain to your staff we'll be sleeping in separate rooms?' she asked. 'It's going to be a paper marriage, remember?'

His unwavering dark gaze made something in her inner core flutter like a baby bird breaking out of its cramped shell. 'We will have to share intimate living spaces—it's what married couples do. I have a large suite in my villa in Milan with a dressing room off the master bedroom. I can sleep there if you'd prefer not to share a bed.'

Frankie's eyes widened. 'Are you out of your mind? There's no way I'm sharing a bedroom suite, no matter how big it is, with you. No flipping way.' She strode off towards the stairs.

'I gave you my word, Francesca. Don't insult me by not believing it.'

Frankie stopped walking and swung back to face him. His expression was difficult to read but she sensed he was disappointed in her lack of trust. It was strange, but she realised she did trust him. She couldn't explain why other than he was the sort of man who could have any woman he wanted, so why would he force himself on someone so unwilling?

But the truth was she wasn't as unwilling as she made out and she had a feeling he knew it. How could she trust she wouldn't end up on his side of the bed, offering herself to him? Begging him to make love to her?

'Why are you doing this? Why? Is it because I rejected your offer of a date all those years ago? Is this your plan for revenge?'

'I'm simply being practical about this, *cara*. People will talk if we don't share a bedroom. I can't guarantee all my staff members will be discreet. I don't wish to encourage such gossip and innuendo at the start of our marriage.' He gave a brief on-off smile that didn't involve his eyes. 'Believe me, you'll thank me for it in the long run.'

Sharing a bedroom with Gabriel Salvetti.

Frankie stood with one hand on the newel post at the bottom of the stairs to keep herself steady. Her legs were feeling wobbly as if her bones were dissolving as images popped into her head of her lying next to him in bed. Not just sharing the suite but sharing a bed. Sharing her body. What if he slept naked? *Gulp.* Heat coursed through her body, traitorous heat that spilled and pooled and scorched. 'Will you find it hard pretending to your staff you're in love with me?' She was proud of the evenness of her tone in spite of the tumult going on inside her flesh.

He shrugged one broad shoulder in a casual manner but his eyes remained screened, inscrutable, secretive. 'It won't be a problem.'

She stepped off the stairs and stood within a metre of him. 'Maybe you should practise saying it.'

Something in his gaze hardened like a computer screen freezing. 'That won't be necessary.'

'I think it is. You need to practise so you sound genuine.' Frankie knew she was playing with fire but so far he'd had the upper hand. She had to even things up a bit. To make herself feel less vulnerable. 'People will expect you to drop those three little words all the time.'

'The words mean nothing without actions.' His eyes flicked to her mouth and back to her gaze with a searing, penetrating gleam. 'Are you suggesting I practise those too?'

He was suddenly close. Not quite touching but close enough for her to want him to. Close enough for her skin to lift in a shiver of anticipation and her breath to stutter in her chest. He glanced at her mouth again, his gaze lingering as long as a passionate kiss. Her lips reacted as if he *had* kissed her. They tingled and tightened and something deep in her core stirred, shifted, stretched.

Frankie forced herself to hold his gaze. 'You're only allowed to touch me with my permission, remember?'

His mouth tilted in a knowing smile, his eyes so dark they looked like glittering pools of black ink. 'You give me permission every time you look at me, *cara*.'

'That sounds like a man with an oversized ego talking.' Frankie's tone was husky—a little too close to flirting husky.

'It's not the size of my ego you need to be worried about.' His voice was a deep burr that did strange fizzing and tingling things to the base of her spine.

Heat exploded in her cheeks, the same heat that was pooling in between her thighs. She arched her brows goaded on by some inner demon of mischief. 'Are you flirting with me, Gabriel?'

He placed his hand on the wall behind her head, caging her on one side but still giving her plenty of room to escape. His gaze homed in on her mouth, the warm minty breeze of his breath skating over her lips like a caress. 'What do you think, *cara*?'

She couldn't think. Not with him this close. Close enough to see the dark individual pinpricks of his stubble. He had shaved since last night but the regrowth was as urgent as the hormones surging in his blood. Hormones that were probably hardening his body right here and now. The hard male body that was so close she could feel the heat coming off him in radiating waves. So close she could press her body against the temptation of his if she wanted to. Which she did. Badly. She wanted it so badly it was like a virulent fever in her blood. A gushing tide of longing that was bursting through the sand bags of her common sense. Ripping apart the tight corset of her self-control.

She ran the tip of her tongue over her lips and watched him follow the movement with his smouldering gaze. 'I think you want to kiss me.' Frankie was a little shocked at how brazen she was being but she couldn't seem to stop herself. The rush of feminine power she was feeling was potently addictive. 'You want to so much.'

His lazy smile made something in her belly turn over. 'Ask me to kiss you and I'll do it but not before.' His voice had a gravel and honey combo going on that made something at the backs of her knees trickle like sand passing through an hourglass.

Frankie dragged in a skittery breath, her heart rate skipping, her self-control slipping. She lowered her lashes to half-mast over her eyes, her gaze trained on the sensual curve of his mouth. *Ask him. Ask him. Ask him.* It was a chant inside her head. A pulsing aching need inside her body. But then, with a willpower she hadn't known she still possessed, she brought her gaze back to meet the challenging heat of his. 'You think I can't resist you. But I can and I will.'

His gaze moved back and forth between her eyes, a searching probe that made her wonder if she had spoken too soon. Too confidently. 'Who exactly are you fighting? Me or yourself?'

Frankie knew she should have moved away from him well before now but she was locked in some sort of weird stasis. His left arm was close enough to her face she could have leaned against his tanned and muscled flesh if she so much as moved an inch or two. She raised her chin and iced her gaze. 'You haven't bought me, Gabriel. Don't *ever* forget that.'

His eyes glinted and he stepped back from her. 'Good to know, *cara*.' And without another word he walked away.

Frankie let out a breath she hadn't been aware of holding. Would there ever be a time when she felt she had won a round with him? He was darn near invincible.

And in less than twenty-four hours he would be her husband.

Frankie didn't see Gabriel for much of that afternoon. She kept herself busy organising extended leave from work, shocking herself at how easily the lies fell from her lips. But what other option did she have? She couldn't risk Gabriel reneging on the deal. There was too much at stake. The money her father owed was being paid back that day now that the paperwork had been signed. She had to accept the situation for what it was—a rescue plan that meant she gave up her freedom for a year.

But what else would she be sacrificing?

How well did she know Gabriel Salvetti? How well did anyone know him? He had a public persona, but how much was that from the press's imagination or speculation and how much of it was true? He had a reputation as a love-them-and-leave-them playboy. Would the public actually believe he had fallen in love with her? She was nothing like his usual type of lover. And why was she using *that* word? She was *not* going to be his lover. She had been adamant their marriage would be on paper only. Of course, he thought she would change her mind. He probably thought she was halfway in love with him already.

But there was no way she would ever be so foolish.

No. Way.

Frankie came downstairs that evening to find Gabriel preparing dinner. There were fresh ingredients on the kitchen island bench as well as various pots and utensils. 'What are you doing?' she asked, frowning. 'I thought you were going to engage a new housekeeper?'

He opened a drawer to search for a chopping board. 'She won't be starting until Monday.' He found the board and rinsed it under the tap. 'I thought we'd stay in tonight. We have a big day tomorrow.'

'Gosh. Lucky me, getting a husband who can cook.' She couldn't quite wipe the sarcasm from her tone.

He dried his hands on a tea towel, his eyes containing a devilish glint. 'Isn't that what most women want? A man who's good with his hands?'

Frankie folded her arms and gave him a look that threatened to wither the fresh basil lying on the bench. 'I thought a man with your amount of wealth wouldn't bother with doing anything domestic. That you'd have servants running after you all the time.'

He began slicing off an onion's skin, his crooked smile fading. 'You know what they say about growing up with too many silver spoons.'

Frankie pulled out one of the kitchen stools to sit opposite him. Is that what he thought she was? A spoilt little rich girl who didn't know her way around a kitchen? 'No. What do they, whoever they are, say?'

He pushed the skin to one side and began chopping the onion like he was a celebrity chef on a cooking show. And surprise, surprise—there wasn't a tear in sight. If that had been Frankie she would have been panda-eyed by now.

'It's not wise to become so waited upon that you become completely useless.' He met her gaze briefly and then reached for a bulb of garlic, expertly separating it into cloves, which he preceded to crush with the flattened blade of the cooking knife.

Frankie chewed at her lower lip. 'Is that how you see me? As a spoilt brat who doesn't know one end of a tea towel from the other?'

He frowned at her injured tone. 'No. Your father told me you're an excellent cook.'

'One of the housekeepers taught me when I was about ten or so. I really missed her when she left.' Frankie shifted her gaze and toyed with the fresh green tops of the bunch of baby carrots lying close to her. 'Who taught you to cook?' She glanced up at him. 'Your mother? One of the servants?'

He picked up another clove of garlic and crushed it with the same dexterity as before. His expression was focused in concentration but she sensed an underlying tension at the mention of his family. 'We didn't have servants until I was twelve.' He picked up the chopping board and used the knife to scrape off the crushed garlic into a small bowl ready for cooking later.

'So, your mother taught you?'

Gabriel rinsed the knife under the tap and then

met her gaze. 'Remember my rule? No questions about my family.'

Frankie frowned. 'Do you think it might be reasonable for me to ask a few questions of the man I'm marrying tomorrow? I hardly know anything about you other than the little my father told me and what I've read in the press.'

He placed his hands on the bench either side of the chopping board, his expression as tightly closed as one of unpeeled onions. After a moment, he let out a harsh-sounding sigh. 'My mother died when I was nine. She was there one minute and then she wasn't. End of story.'

'How did she die?'

The landscape of his face tightened as if every muscle had gone into lockdown. An emotionally parched landscape where no tears would ever be allowed to fall. But a wick of pain briefly flickered in his gaze as if the devastated child he had been was still somewhere deep inside him. Hidden. Hurting. Unhealed.

Gabriel pushed away from the bench and picked up a bottle of red wine he had set out earlier. 'Drink? Or would you prefer white?' His tone was casual. Too casual. Cool and casual masking an undercurrent of raw unspoken grief.

'Red is fine.'

Frankie watched as he poured the wine into the glasses, his movements measured and steady. He handed her a glass of ruby-red pinot noir with a closed-lipped smile. 'Cheers.' He touched his glass against hers and raised his glass to his mouth. He took a sip and his strong tanned throat moved up and down convulsively, as if it wasn't just the wine he was swallowing but something much less palatable. Something thick and rough and choking.

'It's okay, Gabriel,' Frankie said into the silence. 'If you don't want to talk about it then don't. I understand, really I do. I hate talking about my mother. I hate thinking about all I have missed out on in not having her all my life. I hate knowing that my life came at the expense of hers and my twin brother's.'

Gabriel put his glass down on the bench, his gaze suddenly dark with concern. 'No, *cara*. You mustn't blame yourself.' His voice was deep and rough around the edges.

Frankie pushed her own wine glass away and sighed. 'Hard not to when every time I looked at my father I could see how much her death had broken him. I've had to live with it all my life. The crushing, gut-churning guilt. I sometimes wonder if it's my fault he got cancer. All that stress has to do something negative to you, doesn't it?'

He came around to her side of the island bench and took both her hands in his. His thumbs stroked over the back of her hands in a soothing rhythm, his eyes meshing with hers. 'It's not your fault.

None of it. Your father would be sad to hear you blame yourself.'

Frankie looked down at their joined hands, trying to ignore the way her body was reacting to his touch. Her skin felt as if every nerve was on high alert, every muscle and sinew and tendon in her hands vibrating with longing. A longing that travelled deep throughout her body, in her breasts, her belly, between her thighs. She lifted her head, her heart skipping a beat when she made eye contact. The atmosphere crackled with invisible waves of desire. Male desire. Hot urgent male need colliding with restless female hunger.

His gaze went to her mouth, lingered there for a pulsing moment and then came back to her eyes. He gave her hands another quick squeeze and released them, his expression shifting back to neutral as if a mental gear had been clicked into place. 'I'd better get on with this meal. Take your drink out to the terrace. The outdoor heaters are on. I'll join you soon.' His back-to-business tone was jarring given she was so certain just a moment ago he was going to kiss her. Even more jarring was the realisation that she wanted him to.

'Don't you want some help with dinner?' Frankie asked. 'I could slice those mushrooms for you if you—'

'I'm better left alone.' He softened it with a wry smile. 'Too many distractions put me off my game.'

Frankie wandered out to sit on the terrace where the moon was just rising in an egg-yolk-yellow ball, casting a shimmering beam of gold across the water. There was a slight breeze, not cold but with just enough of a chill to make her glad of the warm rays of the gas heaters Gabriel had lit earlier. The looming spires of the majestic mountains beyond the shores of the lake were a rich indigo blue.

How many generations of her family had sat out here and looked at that stunning vista? Had her mother sat here and dreamed of her future? Dreamed of her and her brother?

It was impossible not to feel grateful for what Gabriel had done to save her family home. What he was doing to save her from public humiliation.

But it was also impossible not to worry that the step she was taking tomorrow in becoming his wife for a year was a step on the wrong side of safety.

A step too far.

CHAPTER FIVE

GABRIEL CAME OUT to the terrace once he'd put the meal in the oven to simmer. Frankie was sitting in one of the outdoor chairs facing the view of the moon rising over the lake. She was dressed in dark blue skinny-leg jeans and an emerald green boyfriend sweater that clung to the lush curves of her breasts. Her curly dark brown hair a few shades lighter than his own was scooped up in a casual knot at the back of her head, highlighting the regal length of her neck. She was moon goddess meets girl-next-door and it was all he could do to keep his distance.

It had been a close call inside earlier. He had looked at her plump rose-pink mouth and had to call on every ounce of willpower he possessed not to kiss her. Her cool aloofness had always intrigued him. But he knew beneath that ice princess mask she was a deeply passionate woman. Why she seemed so unwilling to express it made him wonder if something or someone in her past had hurt her. Had she had her heart broken by a past lover?

Her father had been vague about his daughter's love life—not that Gabriel had pressed him too much on it. He had always played it cool when it came to the topic of Frankie. He hadn't wanted to put any silly ideas in Marco Mancini's head about him having a permanent future with his only daughter.

Gabriel wasn't the settling-down-for-ever type. He had seen too much of the heartache of family life to want it for himself. Heartache and mistakes that couldn't be undone. Mistakes he had made—was probably *still* making—with Carli. Why would he invite any more responsibilities into his life?

Frankie must have sensed his presence for she turned her head and smiled. 'It's so beautiful out here. I'd almost forgotten how beautiful…'

Gabriel took the seat next to her, stretching his legs out in front of him. 'I don't suppose you got much time to sit and look at the view over the last couple of months nursing your father.'

She breathed out a jagged sigh, a frown pulling at her forehead. 'No…' Her fingers toyed with the stem of her wine glass. She had only drunk a third of her wine, if that. 'I had help, of course. There was a nurse who came to administer the drugs and help me bathe him.' She turned to glance at him, her frown deepening. 'Why did you only visit him once during that time? And was it deliberate that you timed your visit when I was out doing errands that day?'

Gabriel's visit had been fleeting because of his concerns over Carli, who had been staying with him at his villa in Milan at the time. His little sister had been in one of her down moods and he'd had to judge when or if it was safe to leave her. He currently had no idea where Carli was after yet another failed attempt at an exclusive and expensive eating disorders clinic he'd organised for her in South America. She popped in and out of his life when it suited her and gave little or no regard to the gut-wrenching worry she caused him.

He hadn't been able to get to Marco's Mancini's funeral because Carli had taken an overdose of prescription drugs. She had never done anything so desperate before and it rocked him to the core. He had spent days by her hospital bedside, his sense of failure never more acute. He had paid for the best therapist—one of many he had engaged for her over the years—but she was just as likely to do a no-show at the appointments. Weeks could go by and he would hear nothing and then she would appear and he would have to handle whatever state she was in.

It was the stuff of gut-ripping nightmares.

He shifted his gaze to the view. 'I figured you didn't need me hanging around stealing what little time you had left with him.'

'But you were close to him, weren't you?'

Gabriel lifted one shoulder in a shrug. 'Yes and no. I've always been grateful for his help early in my career and for the nomination for the board last year. We caught up now and again at various business functions and board meetings. But we talked about business, not so much about personal stuff.' He glanced at her and added, 'If he had considered me a close friend, wouldn't he have told me about your twin brother?'

She frowned and nodded as if that made perfect sense. 'I sometimes wonder if he was close to anyone after my mother died.' She gave another sigh. 'He was a hard person to get close to. Even when I hugged him he held me slightly aloof. He had a wall around him. An invisible wall that I could never seem to get through.'

'Perhaps he was always like that,' Gabriel offered. 'Some men find it difficult to express emotion even to those they love.'

'Do you find it difficult?' The moonlight was reflected off her eyes as they met his, making them shimmer like the lake in the distance.

The sound of a message coming in on his phone was perfect timing...or so he thought until he saw his sister's name come up on the screen. He rose from the chair, a chill of unease prickling over his scalp like a flow of iced water. 'Will you excuse me? I have to get this.'

Frankie sipped her wine and tried not to feel disappointed their conversation had been interrupted. Gabriel's insights into her father were comforting on one level. But they didn't stop her feeling she hadn't been enough for her father. Didn't stop her feeling that, if given a choice, her father would have chosen her brother over her.

Gabriel came back out to the terrace. 'I'm sorry, Francesca, but I have to shoot back to Milan tonight.'

Frankie frowned and got to her feet. 'Tonight? Why?'

'Don't worry, I'll be back in time for the ceremony tomorrow.' He gave her an on-off smile that was too fleeting to be the right side of genuine. 'It will give you time to get ready. The celebrant is coming at ten. Dinner is ready—just help yourself. I've turned the oven off.'

She followed him back into the villa. 'But surely whatever it is can wait until Monday. Don't you ever take time off work even to get married?'

He snatched up his car keys from the table in the foyer, his features a road map of tension. 'Some things can't wait. This is one of them. *Ciao.*' And with that he was gone.

Frankie went back to the kitchen but her appetite had deserted her. Just like her father's funeral, she hadn't realised how much she wanted Gabriel to be with her until he wasn't. The villa seemed so empty. Full of shadows and regrets wandering around like lost ghosts.

Gabriel got back to his villa in Milan an hour later to find his sister in situ as if she owned the place. He only hoped she hadn't brought any rag tag mate home with her. It wouldn't be the first time. He had given her a key—one of several which she had promptly lost or given to one of her erstwhile friends. He'd had to change the locks so many times he had the locksmith on speed dial.

Carli turned down the volume of his flat screen television and unfolded her coltish figure from the leather sofa. Coltish was probably too generous a term. She had lost even more weight since the last time he had seen her and he wondered if she was relapsing again. She see-sawed between bingeing and starving and his heart ached to see her unable to enjoy food the way he did. Food was either her friend or her enemy. 'What took you so long?' Her mouth was turned down in a pout that wouldn't have looked out of place on a three-year-old.

'You wouldn't believe me if I told you.' Gabriel tossed his jacket over the back of the sofa. 'But more to the point—where have *you* been? I've been trying to contact you for three weeks. I was about to engage another private investigator.'

Carli's dark brown eyes gleamed with mischief. 'Ooh, please do. I enjoyed the last one. He was absolutely dynamite in bed.'

Gabriel rolled his eyes and headed to the kitchen. 'Have you eaten?' Dumb question. His kitchen looked like a cooking show had got out of hand. Food scraps, packing and dirty dishes were strewn about.

He turned to look at Carli when she followed him into the kitchen. 'By the way, I'm getting married tomorrow.'

Her eyebrows shot up. 'No way. Really? It's not that blonde chick you were seeing when I was in that clinic in Rio? That snooty social worker—what was her name again?'

'No. It's not her.' He couldn't even remember the woman's name now, neither could he recall her features. The trip to get his sister in an expensive clinic was still something he chose not to remember in any detail. Mostly because it had failed and the one thing he hated was failing. Especially when it came to his kid sister. 'It's Francesca Mancini.'

Carli's eyes danced like there were auditioning for the Bolshoi ballet. She pulled out one of the stools and sat down, her ankles wrapping around the base like a vine. 'No joke? Little Miss Ice Princess?'

'I'd prefer you not to call her that.'

She filched a crisp from a packet on the bench and popped it into her mouth. 'So, am I going to meet her?'

'It depends.'

'On what?'

'On whether you can behave yourself.'

His sister scowled at him and tipped the crisp packet upside down so the contents fell out on the bench. She chose another crisp from the pile and bit into it. 'Don't be such a control freak, big bro. I know how to behave.'

Gabriel had seen too much of his sister's behaviour to want to expose Frankie to it. To expose anyone to it. Few people knew he even had a sister. He had gone to great lengths to keep her out of the public eye for her own protection. He was worried that if the press got a photo of Carli during one of her bad phases it would destroy her. But trying to take care for his sister was impossible. He wanted to bang his head against the nearest wall in frustration. He wanted to snap his fingers and have this nightmare over.

He wanted his sister to be normal, happy, healthy. But no matter how hard he tried to help her, she threw it back in his face. She was intent on self-destructing but he couldn't let her do it. He *wouldn't* let her do it.

Not while he still had breath in his body and money in his bank account.

'I worry about you, Carli. I do nothing but worry about you and what do I get in return? You trash my house and abuse my trust when I say anything, you storm off and disappear for weeks or months on end.' He stopped to draw breath, his chest aching with the pressure of years of built-up guilt and regret. He had tried his best to keep his siblings safe. He'd blown it with his younger brothers but Carli was his last chance.

He was *her* last chance.

No one else loved her enough to help her. His father and brothers and cousins were incapable of it.

Carli shrugged as if he'd just told her the latest weather report. 'You worry too much. I can take care of myself.'

He glanced at the fine white scars on her forearms. Thankfully there didn't seem to be any new cuts but how long before there were? 'Do you need a place to stay? I have to go back to Milan tomorrow but I can organise someone to stay with you here if—'

'I'm staying with a friend.'

'Which friend?'

She jumped off the stool she was perched on. 'No one you know.'

Gabriel ground his teeth so hard he mentally apologised to his dentist. His sister's friends were not true friends. They exploited her generosity and her need to belong. 'Will you at least promise me you'll keep in touch? I bought you a top-notch phone the last time but you haven't answered a text or call in—'

'I keep forgetting to charge it.' Her tone was all innocence but her gaze sparkled with a *you-can't-keep-tabs-on-me* defiance.

'Do you need money?' He had lost count of how much he had given her over the years. He had bought her an apartment in Florence when she told him she wanted to live there but she rarely stayed there now. He hadn't decided whether it was a good thing or bad thing to keep giving her funds. But what other choice did he have?

'No. Ricci gave me some.'

Gabriel frowned so hard he thought his face would split right down the middle like a slashed melon. 'I thought you and Ricci weren't in touch any more?' His younger brother was trouble. Even bigger trouble than his other brother Lorenzo. Was there no end to this nightmare of his freaking family?

'I ran into him in Palermo,' Carli said. 'He said to say hi.'

'Carli, listen to me.' He placed his hands on her shoulders locking her gaze with his. 'You have to stay away from Ricci and Lorenzo and Papa. Promise me. Don't have any contact with them.

No texts. No calls. No visits back home to Sicily. Nothing.'

Her hazel eyes shimmered. 'Everyone needs a family, Gabriel. Even you.'

'You don't need them.' He squeezed her shoulders and then pulled her into a tight hug. 'I'm your family, *mio piccolo*. Always remember that.'

CHAPTER SIX

FRANKIE WOKE ON the morning of her wedding day to bright sunshine slanting through the gap in the curtains. She hoped it was a good omen. But what was positive about marrying a man for the sake of convenience? A man she was beginning to realise was complex, deep and mysterious. A man who, by just looking at her, made her flesh sing.

She threw off the bedcovers and pulled the curtains all the way back so she could take in the view. Rich autumn colours—red, gold, rust, orange, yellow, burgundy—adorned the deciduous trees. And because it was so peaceful and still, the smooth silver surface of the lake provided a perfect reflection of the bold and glorious hues.

Frankie sighed and turned to glance at her mother's wedding dress hanging where she had left it last night. It seemed strange to be preparing for her wedding on her own. Strange, but not atypical for didn't she spend most of her time feeling alone and isolated?

Gabriel had texted her the details of the arrangements for the day. There would be a short ceremony in the garden with just the celebrant and a photographer and his partner as witness, and they would fly to the south of France the following morning for a short honeymoon. Gabriel had organised the marriage license ahead of time to comply with Italian law, which made Frankie realise he had been completely confident she would marry him right from the start. How did she get to be so predictable?

Why had he rushed off last night? What could have been so important? He had a reputation as a hard-working businessman. Did he use work to make up for the shame he felt about his family? Shame she could sense in him, although he point-blank refused to speak about them.

Frankie showered and washed and dried her hair, fashioning it into an up-do on her head. It was not as sophisticated as it would have been if she had been waited on by a hairdresser, but the circumstances of their marriage made it seem unnecessary to hire professional hair and makeup artists for the sake of a short impersonal ceremony.

She applied her makeup and sprayed her favourite perfume on her wrists and neck. She didn't have much jewellery with her, only the engagement ring and the pearl studs she wore most of the time. She had sold her heirloom jewels—they had been yet another casualty of her desperate financial circumstances.

Frankie heard cars arriving and glanced out of the window to see who she presumed was the celebrant as well as a photographer and his female partner. Close behind was Gabriel's sports car. She couldn't stop herself from drinking in the sight of him as he got out of the car and greeted the others. His top-shelf gunmetal-grey suit, white shirt and blue tie marked him as a successful and sophisticated man about town. His hair was brushed back from his forehead, his face clean-shaven, and she wondered if she'd ever seen a more dashing-looking bridegroom.

Her bridegroom.

When it was time for her to go downstairs, Gabriel sent her a text. It seemed he was something of a traditionalist in that he hadn't come up to see her in her dress before the ceremony.

Frankie came out of her bedroom and walked down the grand staircase to where he was waiting below. When he first caught sight of her, he looked slightly stunned. His eyes widening, his throat rising and falling. 'You look beautiful...' Even his voice had a shocked quality to it and when he took her hand in his, she was sure his was shaking. Or maybe that was hers. Her heart gave a nervous flutter as his fingers curled around hers.

'Thank you.' Frankie felt suddenly shy.

'I thought it would be nice to walk out to the garden together,' Gabriel said. 'The celebrant and photographer and his partner are waiting there now.'

Frankie drew in a calming breath. 'Okay. Let's do it then.'

'Are you feeling nervous?' His gentle tone ambushed her, making her wonder if he too was feeling the same. But why would he? He wasn't the vulnerable one.

He was the one with all the power and control.

She shifted her gaze to focus on the Windsor knot of his tie. 'A little… It's not every day I get to marry someone I have only met a handful of times.'

He tipped up her face with his finger to lock her gaze with his. His brown eyes were warm and surprisingly earnest. 'You have no need to feel afraid. We will get to know each other in time.'

But would a year be long enough?

Gabriel led Frankie out into the sunshine of the garden where the celebrant and photographer and his partner were waiting. He had kept the press away on purpose—he would make a formal announcement once he and Frankie were officially married. He hadn't wanted any members of his family showing up or press drones flying overhead.

He wanted the ceremony to be in keeping with

what their marriage would ultimately be—simple and brief. Unsentimental.

But it had been difficult to keep his sentiments in check when he had first caught sight of her coming down the stairs toward him. Her mother's dress was an exquisite lace and silk affair with a voluminous skirt and a classic veil held in place with a princess tiara. With her creamy elegantly made-up skin and her glossy dark hair in a stylish bun and her lips painted a cherry red, she looked like a fairy tale character—Sleeping Beauty come to vibrant, stunning life. He had never seen a more breathtakingly beautiful bride.

Gabriel stood with Frankie in front of the celebrant and the ceremony began. 'We are gathered here today…'

Gabriel had been to plenty of weddings before and knew the drill almost verbatim. But it was so different being the groom, holding the hand of his bride and placing the ring on her finger. Hearing her softly but clearly saying the vows that tied her to him. Gabriel wasn't a religious man by any means, but there was something sacred about the moment—looking into her grey-blue eyes and hearing her promise to love him.

To worship him with her body.

To allow him to honour and protect her.

It was a bold promise on his part. Rash even. But it hadn't sat well with him for her to lose her inheritance. He was honouring her father by marrying her, by rescuing her from certain bankruptcy and public humiliation. Apart from his concerns over his business reputation, there were no other motivations for marrying her other than doing the right thing by the man who had put his own prejudice aside and given him a chance to leave his background behind.

'You may kiss the bride.'

Gabriel lowered his mouth to Frankie's, pausing for an infinitesimal moment before he touched his lips to hers. Any thought of a brief brush of his lips against hers was lost in the first point of contact. Her mouth was as soft as a rose petal and she tasted of cherries, and as he drew away her lips clung to his as if they couldn't bear to part from his. He pressed his mouth back down on hers, firmer, moulding his lips to the sweet sensual curve of hers, and a rumble of longing swept through him to burn and pulse and pound in his groin.

She gave a soft, breathless little sound, a sound of approval and encouragement, a sound of breathless female desire, and it made the blood in his veins thicken and thrum and thunder. He slipped one of his hands to the nape of her neck, angling his head to deepen the kiss, the need so powerful, so uncontrollable it took him completely by surprise. Kissing her was like tasting an irresistible drug for the first time, an addictive, mind-altering potion that left his senses spinning, singing, shrieking.

The whir of the photographer's camera shutter was the only thing that jolted Gabriel out of the kiss. He'd been captivated by kisses before, but not enough to forget where he was. To forget everything but the taste and texture and temptation of Frankie's mouth and the overwhelming longing to do much more than kiss her.

He lifted his head away from hers, more than a little delighted she looked as stunned as he felt. Her eyes were bluer than grey, darkened with the same desire he could feel rocketing through his blood. Her breathing was a little uneven, her mouth still slightly open, and he seriously wondered if he would ever be able to look at a cherry again without thinking of the sweet fresh taste of her mouth.

Frankie gave him a tremulous smile. 'I wasn't expecting that…'

'Should I have asked permission first?' Gabriel knew he sounded faintly mocking but he didn't want her to think he was in any way undone by that kiss. Or a little undone by the fact he now was officially bound to her in marriage. A *temporary* marriage, but still. The M and C words—marriage and commitment—were ones he had actively avoided during his adult life. He had avoided intimate relationships that had certain expectations, responsibilities and emotional ties that couldn't easily be severed.

Something flickered in her gaze—a flash of disappointment? A shadow of hurt? She lowered her eyes to stare at his chin. 'I'm sure there will be times when we both have to do things we would rather not do for the sake of appearances.'

Gabriel took her hands and gently squeezed them. 'We will have a short photo session after we sign the register and then we will be alone. Grin and bear it, *cara*, for before you know it the year will be up.'

After the photos were taken and the paperwork completed, Frankie picked up a glass of champagne and downed it in three gulps. She couldn't get Gabriel's kiss out of her mind. She could still taste him. Could still feel the firm warm pressure of his lips against hers. Could still feel the humming and thrumming of her blood—the heady rush of desire his mouth had triggered in her body. Her traitorous, wilfully disobedient body that refused to listen to the sensible and rational part of her brain.

For a moment during the ceremony she'd thought he had been as taken aback as her by their kiss. The meeting of their mouths had been like two planets colliding. Sparks had fired in her blood, tingles had shot down her legs, heat had pooled and simmered and smouldered in her core.

Had she imagined his reaction? It wasn't as if she had a lot of experience when it came to reading a man's response to her. She had been kissed before but no kiss had ever had that effect on her. To make her so unaware of her surroundings, unaware of the two witnesses standing close by, so unaware of anything but the feel of Gabriel's lips exploring hers.

Gabriel saw off the celebrant and the photographer and his partner and came back to Frankie. 'We will leave for France from Milan first thing in the morning. I'm afraid there will be some press attention—I need it to make sure my business interests are well served. The news of our marriage will be hot news for a while but hopefully it won't last long.'

Frankie turned to refill her champagne glass and then looked back at him again. 'Just like our marriage, huh? A flash-in-the-pan affair. Blink and you'll miss it.' She raised her glass to her mouth and took another generous sip. 'Go us.'

Gabriel took the glass out of her hand and placed it back on the table, a frown carving into his forehead. 'Francesca, I understand a day such as today is likely to stir emotions in you but let me be clear again. This is temporary because that's what I believe is fair to you in the long run. You're young enough to marry again once we're done.'

Once we're done. Such cold, clinical words. Just

like the ceremony…apart from that disturbingly addictive kiss. Maybe it had been a mistake to drink that champagne so fast—it was loosening her tongue and her emotions. Making her think of things, yearnings and wishes she had no right to be thinking. It was all laid out in his contract.

One year of marriage.

No promises of for ever. No promises of a family. *No love.*

Frankie gave a disingenuous smile. 'Oh, did you think I was complaining? What's to complain about? You've spent a virtual fortune getting me out of a financial mess and saved me from public humiliation by marrying me. Thank you, by the way.' She mock-frowned and placed a finger against her chin in a musing pose. 'Did I thank you before?'

He released a breath in a steady stream as if he was mentally counting to ten. 'You are tired and overwrought. It's been a big couple of days and—'

'How are we going to explain our relationship? How we met and so on? How you proposed?' She gave a coy smile and placed her index finger at the top of his tie and sent it down in a slow journey to the middle of his concrete-hard abdomen, turning her fingertip in a lazy circle. 'How we fell in *lurve.*'

His eyes became as hard as two black bolts and he captured her hand, his fingers wrapping around hers like steel. 'I know what you're trying to do but it won't work.'

Frankie looked at him through lashes lowered to half-mast. *Who knew she could do seductive siren so well?* His firm hold and implacable stance was doing something strange to her. Making her bold and brazen and reckless. Unleashing a wildness in her like releasing a long-caged beast.

Making her *want*.

She wasn't a flirter and look what she was doing—flirting. Enjoying every moment of it. Enjoying the sense of power it gave her to know he was not as immune to her as he made out. That kiss had told her how much he was attracted to her.

'What am I doing, hmm?' She moved closer to him, drawn to him like a teensy little iron filing to a powerful magnet. 'Are you worried you might lose control of yourself, my dark angel Gabriel?'

He drew in a harsh breath, his eyes blazing with heat. With hot male desire. 'If you want to make our marriage a physical one all you have to do is ask.' His voice was a deep rough burr that made her inner core contract with longing.

Frankie placed her free hand on his chest, her lower body so close to him she could feel the surge of him against her belly. It was shockingly intimate. The most intimate she had been with a man since she was a teenager. But back then she had pulled away, unable to take it any further. Unwilling to give herself to someone who only saw her as a trophy to collect. But now she was a woman, an adult woman with a desperate need to explore a man's body.

Gabriel's body.

Her husband.

The rush of alcohol left Frankie's system as fast as it had hit it only moments earlier. What was she doing? Could she really contemplate giving herself to him for the loveless year of their marriage? Could she risk opening herself up to hurt by allowing him *that* close to her? Hadn't his kiss already shown her how dangerous it was to let her guard down? He made her feel things she didn't want to feel. She couldn't allow herself to feel vulnerable. Couldn't allow herself to want what other people took for granted.

Love. Intimacy. *Belonging.*

Those were the things were other people deserved, not her.

Frankie pulled out of his hold and gave him a lopsided smile. 'Maybe I'll get back to you on that.'

'Take your time.' If he was disappointed in her answer nothing in his tone or his expression showed it.

Gabriel sat in the library later that evening sorting through emails and messages on his phone. Frankie had gone upstairs after their conversation and he hadn't gone in search of her since. Hadn't been game enough to in case his resolve took another sucker punch. He knew he could have talked her into sleeping with him. She had been feeling conflicted about their marriage, about the step they had taken today. Her emotions were all over the place and what sort of man would he be if he took advantage of her in such a vulnerable state?

But it had felt damn good to kiss her. To touch her. To hold her. He wanted her with a tight restless ache deep in his body. Thank God he was a patient man. He had no interest in rushing Frankie into bed unless he was absolutely sure it was where she wanted to be. He didn't want her to come back at him at a later date and accuse him of exploiting the situation for his own gain. He was taking the higher ground because that made him more comfortable with how things had panned out. He had saved her from financial ruin, saved her father's reputation, saved her heritage.

Saved himself.

Their marriage was, after all, a business arrangement. A mutually satisfying arrangement that killed two birds with one very powerful stone.

No, he would wait until she came to him. He knew deep in his bones she would. The same way he knew she had wanted to date him four years ago but her pride had got in the way. In a perverse way it had secretly delighted him when she'd rebuffed him. It galvanised him on a mission to prove what he was capable of, what he could do even though he had the dark stain of criminality in his background. He had doubled his wealth in the four years since she'd looked down her noble nose at him, as if he had just crawled out of a swamp with his knuckles dragging. He had built an empire bigger than anything his father had done and he at least had the satisfaction to know that his rise to the top was not over the backs of innocent victims. He had exploited no one, abused the trust of no one, destroyed no one to get where he was today.

And one day soon, very soon, he would claim what he had coveted for all that time—Frankie.

CHAPTER SEVEN

FRANKIE SPENT THE rest of the day moping about
her room, wondering if there had ever been a more
dissatisfied bride on her wedding day. She had
changed out of her mother's dress and hung it back
in the wardrobe, feeling as if she had put on a cos-
tume in a drama. She had walked on set for her
part and now she was back to being herself.

Alone.

Except now she had a new name—Francesca
Antonietta Salvetti. Had she made a terrible mistake? Marrying a man for the sake of rescuing her
heritage? To save herself from financial ruin? A
man she was finding it harder and harder to resist. A man who claimed he would never love her
and would only tie himself to her for a year. Her
clumsy attempt to seduce him had shown her how
truly vulnerable she was. He would not touch her
until she asked and she was determined *not* to ask.
Not to beg. Not to own the treacherous impulses
she was feeling. For it would be the ultimate hu-

miliation to fall for him. He had laid down the rules. This was a business marriage. A contract. An emotionless contract.

And tomorrow they would travel to France for a honeymoon. *A honeymoon*. The words triggered those traitorous urgings again. His kiss during the ceremony had shown her a hint of the passion that simmered between them. A passion that was as addictive as it was disturbing. Disturbing, because she wasn't sure she could control her response to him. She ached to be close to him. His kiss had awakened a burning need in her that refused to go away. She touched her lips with her fingers, tracing where his lips had pressed and caressed and teased and tempted.

Frankie sighed and let her hand fall back by her side. She had to get a grip. Their marriage was only hours old. It wouldn't do her pride any favours for her to be offering herself to him like a prize he'd bought.

She was *not* for sale.

When Frankie came downstairs later that evening, she caught a glimpse of Gabriel out on the terrace. She stood at the French doors without opening them to go out to him. He was speaking on the phone, a frown pulling at his brow, and while she couldn't hear the words from inside the house, she got the impression he was furiously angry with whoever was on the other end of the line. He paced the terrace, back and forth like a lion in too small a cage. His hand speared through his hair, leaving it sexily dishevelled, making her want to trail her fingers through those ink-black strands.

He finished the call with what looked like a muttered expletive and turned and saw her watching him. He slipped the phone in his trouser pocket and came over to open the French door, his expression still taut with tension. He came in and closed the door behind him. 'Sorry. I didn't realise you were there. I thought you were resting upstairs.'

'Is everything all right?'

A mask came down on his features. '*Sì*. Ready for dinner?' His brief smile lacked enthusiasm and she wondered if he ever took a break from business. He seemed distracted and tense even though he was mostly doing a fine job of disguising it. But she was becoming better at reading him. She was better at interpreting the micro expressions on his face, the subtle body language cues that hinted at the complexity of his personality, the mysterious depth and layers.

'Surely you haven't been cooking on your wedding day?' Frankie wished now she had thought to come down and sort dinner out herself.

'I've booked a table at Antonio's. There's a private room so we won't be disturbed by the press or the public.'

She frowned. 'But don't you want the press to find out about our marriage? I thought that was the whole point?'

His eyes held hers for a beat. 'I haven't made the announcement yet. I thought you might need a little extra time before we go public.'

Frankie chewed at her lip, her fingers toying with her wedding and engagement rings on her left hand, to remind herself that, yes, she was actually married to this most enigmatic man. 'Who was on the phone just then?'

Something at the back of his eyes hardened like frost. 'No one important.'

Frankie's stomach pitched. What if he was doing the ring around to all his previous lovers? Letting them know he was off the market before the news became public. That was, *if* he kept himself off the market. What if he didn't? What if he maintained his playboy lifestyle even though they were married? Jealousy rose in her like a tide, filling her with bitter bile. A toxic and painful reminder of how different their relationship was from that of any other recently married couple.

Could she trust him to keep his word? She had trusted people before and look how that had turned out. She had been humiliated time and time again. She frosted her own eyes and her tone. 'Let's hope they stay unimportant for the next twelve months.'

A muscle flicked on and off in his jaw like a

miniature hammer tapping beneath his tanned skin. *Tippety-tap. Tippety-tap.* 'What are you suggesting? That I won't honour the promises I made to you today?'

Frankie turned away from him but she only got two steps before his hand came down on her forearm, turning her back to face him. 'I asked you a question.'

She glanced at his hand on her arm before meeting his stern gaze, injecting her voice with icy hauteur. 'You're touching me.'

A satirical light came into his eyes. 'Isn't that what husbands do to their wives?' His tone was both smooth and rough—gravel and honey rolled together—making her resolve to resist him almost throw up its hands in defeat. How could it be possible to *feel* his voice inside her body? To feel its deep burring echo in all her secret places?

Her heart skipped a beat. Two beats. Her breathing coming to a screeching halt. The air crackled with electricity, pulsing, throbbing with erotic undertones like the bass notes in a chord.

'Not this wife.' Frankie was proud of the stridency of her tone. Of her willpower. Of her *I-can-resist-you* award-winning performance.

Gabriel stroked a lazy finger down the slope of her burning cheek, his eyes so black she couldn't make out the circles of his pupils. 'You like it when I touch you.'

Frankie couldn't quite suppress a shiver of reaction. 'We made an agreement.' Her voice came out so husky she could have been snacking on emery boards.

His finger traced the outline of her mouth, setting off tingling, buzzing, *wanting* in her lips. 'And I'll honour that agreement if you stop looking at me like that.'

She did her best to school her features into bland impassivity. 'How am I looking at you?'

He gave a soft sound of amusement and his finger tipped up her chin so she couldn't escape the penetrating scrutiny of his gaze. 'You want me to kiss you, don't you?'

'I do not.' Frankie's tone was so tart it could have curdled milk. But her breathing was out of control—hectic, shallow, desperate.

His hand cupped the right side of her face, his thumb moving back and forth across her cheek like the arm of a slow-moving metronome. 'I've spent years imagining how it would feel to kiss your beautiful mouth.'

He had? At least she hadn't been the only one with an overactive imagination. 'I hope you weren't disappointed?' Frankie tried to keep the insecurity out of her tone and her expression.

Gabriel stroked his thumb over her bottom lip, his touch as soft as a feather, but it triggered a tumult of sensation in her flesh that travelled all the way to her core. 'Why would you think that?' A frown tugged at his forehead.

She shrugged one shoulder and lowered her lashes over her eyes. 'I'm not exactly your usual type, am I?'

He bumped up her chin once more to lock his gaze with hers. 'My type is someone who responds to me with enthusiasm and enjoyment.'

'I can't imagine there would be any woman who wouldn't respond to you with enjoyment and enthusiasm.' Frankie glanced at his mouth and exhaled a fluttery breath, her voice coming out slightly breathless. 'You're very good at it. Kissing, I mean.'

His eyes went to her mouth, his hand on the side of her face stilling as if deciding whether to release her or bring her closer to him. Frankie made the decision for him by closing the distance between their bodies, pulled by a magnetic force she couldn't withstand. She planted her hands on his chest, one over the thud, thud, thud of his heart. Her body touching him from hip to hip, thigh to thigh, need to need. Male to female.

'Say it, *cara*.' His voice had that deep rough edge again, the edge that made her insides twist and coil with desire. She could feel his body responding to her closeness, the primal surge of his male flesh stirring her senses into a frenzy.

Frankie swept her tongue across her lips, her

gaze focused on the firm contours of his mouth. 'Kiss me, Gabriel.' Her words came out as a whispered plea.

He made a sound that was part-groan, part-growl and covered her mouth with his. Heat exploded in her body when his lips contacted hers. Smouldering, blistering heat that flashed through her flesh like hungry tongues of flame. His lips played with hers in a series of presses and bumps and nudges, ramping up her need like he was stoking a fire.

She opened her mouth under his and released a breathless sigh of pleasure when his tongue boldly mated with hers. A shiver cascaded down her spine when he placed his hands on her hips and drew her even closer to his hot hard heat. Her body ached for him. Ached and pulsed with a deep throb of longing that was as shocking to her as it was exciting. She hadn't thought her body capable of such intense feelings, hadn't thought it capable of such primitive urgings that pushed aside all her earlier reasons for keeping her distance like someone knocking down a house of cards. How could she have ever thought she could resist him?

Gabriel slid one of his hands beneath her hair, the sensitive skin of her nape tingling from his touch. The other hand he placed on the curve of her bottom, pressing her harder against his need. He angled his head and deepened the kiss, sending her into raptures by the spine-tingling expertise of his lips and tongue. It was mesmerising magic to have his mouth on hers, his tongue playing with hers in an erotic dance that made her blood zip and sing through her veins. It was magic to feel the throb of his blood against her, the potent heat of him thrilling her, exciting her, tempting her beyond her control.

After a moment, he raised his head to look at her with his gaze black with desire. Or was that a gleam of victory? A glint of *gotcha*? 'You have no idea how much I want you.'

Frankie pushed back against him to separate their tightly pressed bodies. The self-denial was as painful to her as the shame of being so predictable. He had been so confident she would beg him to make love to her. So arrogantly confident. The ink was barely dry on their contract hands-off marriage and here she was making out with him like a desperate wanton. 'I'm not ready for this. It's…it's not what I want.' She was ashamed of the waver in her voice. Ashamed and annoyed she was so being transparent.

'Fine.' His voice was so calm he could have been discussing the weather. Didn't he feel the least bit frustrated? Was she *that* resistible? She could feel her own frustration clawing at her, rebuking her for pushing him away when her body ached so badly for his possession.

He finger-combed his hair where her fingers had mussed it up during their kiss. She had barely registered she had done it at the time being so caught up in the moment, caught up in the heat and thrill and excitement of his mouth claiming hers.

Frankie rolled her lips together—they were still tingling from his kiss. She could still taste him. Could still *feel* him even though he had put even more distance between them. 'You're not…disappointed?'

He shrugged, his expression as unreadable as a blank page. 'It's your call, *cara*. I told you that from the outset.'

Frankie brought her arms across her middle, trying to keep from reaching for him. 'I hope you don't think I'm a prude or uptight about sex or something…' She kept her gaze averted, worried he would see far more than she wanted him to see.

'Casual sex isn't for everyone.'

She brought her gaze back up to meet his. 'But if we… I mean, would it be casual? We're married so—'

'But only for a year.' His gaze remained steady and frustratingly inscrutable.

She nibbled at her lower lip. 'How long was your longest relationship?'

His mouth slanted in a rueful smile. 'I'm not a fan of long-term relationships.'

'But what was your longest?'

A flicker of frustration passed through his gaze. 'Look, I know the press make out I have a revolving door in my penthouse, but I always make it clear to the women I date what's on offer.'

'Sex without strings.'

'Pretty much.' The tight set of his mouth told her the subject was off limits. He flicked back his sleeve to glance at his watch. 'We should make a move or we'll lose our booking at the restaurant.'

'I'll need to change into something more appropriate.'

His gaze ran over her casual jeans, white shirt and lightweight baby blue cotton blend jumper. 'You look beautiful.'

Frankie could feel her cheeks growing warm. How many times had so-called friends said lovely things only for her to find out they weren't genuine? 'I've seen the photos of the women you date and I can safely say I am not in the same beauty league as them.'

'You're too hard on yourself, *cara*. I think you're one of the most beautiful women I've ever met.' His gaze drifted to her mouth and then back to her gaze. 'Why are you frowning?'

Frankie shifted her body slightly so she wasn't facing him straight on. 'Compliments confuse me. I'm never sure if they're genuine or not.'

He touched her lightly on the shoulder and she turned back to look at him. His forehead was etched in a frown. 'Why do you think like that? Has someone hurt you in the past?'

Frankie was touched by the concern in his gaze. There had been too few people in her life who had actually cared about how she felt. 'It was hard growing up without a mother. Mothers are the ones that build up a kid's confidence. Dads too, but mine was not the demonstrative type. And he was grieving for most of my childhood, which didn't help. He spoilt me in terms of gifts and possessions and holidays but I got the sense he couldn't bear to look at me sometimes. And he certainly never complimented me. I was a constant reminder of what he had lost.'

She released a breath and continued, 'During my teens, I never knew who was my friend because they liked me or the wealthy lifestyle I had. I got caught out more times than I'd like to admit. It was embarrassing. And deeply hurtful.'

Gabriel took both of her hands in his, stroking the backs of them with his thumbs. 'People can be so cruel but it's mostly because they feel inadequate in some way. Broken people break other people to make themselves feel less damaged.'

'Is that what your father is like?'

His thumbs stilled their caressing strokes as if the mention of his father made him uneasy. His gaze became shadowed, closed off. Then he released her hands and stretched his mouth into a brief smile. 'Let's go and have dinner.'

Frankie hesitated. 'Do I have time to get changed? I'd rather be dressed in something more upmarket that jeans.'

'Of course. I'll do the same.'

The restaurant was situated on the shore of Lake Como and the views of the water and the mountains beyond was nothing less than magnificent. Grand villas, similar to Frankie's home, lined the shore on every side and now that it was evening, the glittering lights were reflected in the lake like scattered gold.

The maître d' welcomed them and led them to a private room upstairs decorated in burgundy and black and gold. The plush velvet high-backed chairs, the polished walnut table dressed with a white starched linen tablecloth, fresh flowers and crystal candelabra and glassware and silver cutlery gave the room and the setting a royal residence feel. It made her glad she had got changed into something more glamorous.

Gabriel was wearing a dark blue suit teamed with a lighter shade of blue shirt and a grey and blue striped tie, and looked so strikingly handsome her breath caught every time she looked at him. Her smoky grey satin cocktail dress and matching pashmina and spiky heels at least gave her some measure of confidence that people looking at them would not think her too unworthy to be his dinner date.

Once they were seated with drinks in front of them, Frankie covertly watched Gabriel as he studied the menu. He was very good at concealing his emotions but she sensed he was mulling over something. The mention of his father perhaps? She knew he didn't want to discuss his family but since she had shared so much about her childhood—things she had told virtually no one before—she felt it was only fair he revealed a little about his past.

His forehead was creased in a frown, his dark gaze homed in on the menu, but now and again she saw the way he tensed his jaw. It may have been an unconscious gesture but each time he did it, the fine white scar on his cheekbone became more noticeable.

Frankie took another sip of her wine before asking, 'How did you get that scar?'

He lowered the menu and absently touched his cheekbone with one of his fingers. 'This?' He twisted his mouth but it wasn't really a smile. 'From a fight when I was younger.'

'How old were you?'

He put the menu down and picked up his glass of wine but he didn't bring it to his mouth. He looked into the blood-red contents of his glass, his frown deepening. 'I had just turned eighteen.' He took a mouthful of wine and then put the glass back down. 'It's not a day I'm particularly fond of recalling.'

'Who were you fighting?'

His gaze met hers. 'My father.'

Frankie gasped and clasped a hand to her throat. 'Your father gave you that scar?'

Gabriel's eyes hardened as if the very mention of his father made everything in him turn to stone. 'Yep. Not exactly father of the year material, my old man, but there you go.'

Frankie swallowed. 'What were you fighting about?'

His gaze moved to the base of his wine glass, his fingers pushing it away in a precise movement. He looked back at her with a brooding grimace, something in his gaze shifting as if he had come to some sort of resignation. 'I didn't like the way my father earned a living. I didn't find out what he was actually involved in until my eighteenth birthday when he asked me to join the company.' He put his fingers up in air quotes over the word 'company.' 'He figured I was an adult by then and would have no qualms about breaking the law.'

Frankie opened and closed her mouth in shock. 'So, he hit you when you refused to work with him?'

'Violence is my father's language,' he said in

a grim tone. 'He uses his fists or employs others to do it for him.' He touched the scar again. 'But, yes, this was his handiwork.'

'Oh, Gabriel… I'm so shocked and sad that you have such an appalling father. And here I am complaining about mine. I'm so sorry for dumping all my stuff on you. You must think me a spoilt, overly indulged brat.'

He reached across the table and captured her hand. 'Don't apologise. I know it wasn't easy with your father. He was a good man, a decent man, but he had his faults.'

Frankie placed her other hand on top of his where it was holding hers to the table. 'Was your father ever violent towards your mother?'

He pulled his hand from between hers and leaned back in his chair, his expression clouding once more. 'She got the occasional black eye and once she had to have a cast on her arm. She always had an excuse for how she got hurt. She slipped, walked into a door or whatever. As a child you don't really question it, or at least I didn't back then.' He sighed and added, 'There was a lot I didn't question back then.'

'You didn't witness the violence?'

'I was only nine when she died so it's hard to recall what went on behind closed doors. They didn't seem to argue much but that was probably because my mother knew better than to disagree with him.' He released a savage-sounding sigh. 'It wasn't an easy life for her. We had no money—that came later, after she had died. She did her best to provide for us but the constant struggle for food and taking care of four kids and a difficult husband took its toll.'

'How did she die?'

A flash of something dark and angry backlit his gaze. 'For years we were told it was suicide. But on the day of my eighteenth the truth came out. He had given her drugs to stop her from reporting him to the police. Strong painkillers that shut down her breathing. No one questioned it as anything but an intentional overdose.' A shadow passed over his face as if he was recalling that terrible day. Her heart ached for him. Ached for the small child he had been and how hard and cruel life had been towards him.

'Oh, Gabriel… How awful for you,' Frankie said. 'You must have felt so devastated to lose her. And your poor siblings. They're younger than you, yes?'

'Yes.' He picked up his wine and took a mouthful but when he put the glass back down his expression got that boxed-up look about it again. 'I hate talking about this stuff.'

'I can imagine it must be dreadfully painful.'

A silence passed.

Gabriel's gaze met hers. 'I torture myself with

the what-ifs. What if *I* had come home earlier from school? I might have been able to save her. Get her to hospital in time.'

Frankie's chest was tight with emotion. How sad that, like her, he blamed himself for his mother's death. 'But you were just a child. That's your father's guilt to own, not yours.'

He moved his mouth in a semblance of a smile and took her hand, his thumb toying with the diamonds on her engagement ring. 'I tried to make it up to my mother by taking care of my siblings. I had to grow up damn fast. I can't really recall hanging out with my friends or kicking a ball after school. There were months on end when I didn't even go to school. My father got a new partner after what I thought was an indecently short space of time. One of many women who came and went over the years.'

Frankie was starting to understand why Gabriel was such a closed book when it came to his past. It was so painful to revisit it. To talk about it. To vocalise the intense sadness and loss that had stained his existence. And the guilt, which she understood more than most. She stroked the back of his hand where it was holding hers. 'Thank you for telling me about your past. It helps me to get a clearer picture of who you are. You've always seemed to me a little aloof and unknowable.'

'Is that why you refused to have dinner with

me four years ago?' There was a teasing glint in his eyes.

Frankie pulled her hand away and leaned back from the table, shooting him a mock-reproving look from beneath her lashes. 'I was annoyed that you expected me to say yes. I thought you were unbearably arrogant.'

He gave a self-deprecating smile. 'It was good for me to get a knock back. It made me all the more determined to win you over eventually.'

Frankie frowned. 'But you never asked me again. Not until two days ago, I mean. I might have got married to someone else and had a bunch of kids in the meantime.'

'There are inherent risks in every decision one makes,' he said with an enigmatic smile. 'But lucky for me you were still single and in need of a rich husband.'

Frankie cleared her throat in a theatrical fashion. 'Ahem. Here's a little newsflash for you. I did not *want* a rich husband.' She sent him a glare that would have made a swarm of wasps duck for cover. 'A man's bank balance is not their most attractive feature. Not in my books anyway.'

'What sort of men have you dated?'

Frankie forced herself to hold his unwavering gaze. 'I hope you're not one of those men who has to know every single detail about a woman's sexual past?'

'Not unless there is something about her past that could have an impact on her present.'

Frankie could feel her cheeks starting to glow but she somehow managed to maintain eye contact. 'How many partners have you had? A rough guess will do.'

'Not as many as you might think.'

She raised her eyebrows. 'You've hardly been living like a monk, though, have you? You're always in the gossip pages with yet another gorgeous woman hanging off your arm.'

'They don't always end up in my bed or at least not for long.' A frown flickered across his forehead and he picked up his wine glass and took another sip.

'So, you've never fallen in love?'

'No.'

'Because you've not met the right woman or because you don't want to fall for anyone?'

It was hard to read his expression. The screen had come back up. 'I'm not incapable of loving someone, I just chose not to love an intimate partner in that way.'

'But is it something you *can* choose? Don't you think falling in love is something that just happens? It's not something you can control, surely?'

His gaze hardened with cynicism. 'I've controlled it so far.'

Frankie couldn't hold his gaze and focused on

watching her index finger leave a pathway through the condensation on her water glass. 'I've never been in love either. I've had the odd crush but that's as far as it went.' He was silent so long, she glanced up to find him watching her with a frowning expression. 'What? Why are you looking at me like that?'

'I meant what I said the other day, Francesca.' His tone had a note of gravitas. 'No matter if we end up consummating our marriage or not, this is temporary. *We* are temporary.' She didn't care for the way he leant on the word 'we.' Was it so impossible that he could end up feeling something for her? Something more than temporary lust?

Frankie gave him an arch look. 'I'm not sure why you find it so necessary to keep reminding me. Perhaps it's because you need to keep reminding yourself?'

He held her gaze in silent combat that made the base of her spine tingle. She was determined not to look away. Not to back down from this battle of wills. But as every pulsing second passed she could feel her resolve weakening.

The longer she looked into his cynical dark gaze the more she worried he would see her nascent feelings for him. Feelings she had no control over. Feelings that were growing, changing, evolving into something she had never felt for anyone before. She had shared some of her deepest pain with him and he had shared his. It had created a connection between them—an emotional connection that made it hard for her to dislike him any more.

In fact, she admired him all the more for what he had gone through. How could she not? He was a man who had risen out of the depths of despair and loss and turned his life into a success, not a *poor me* sob story. He was strong and yet gentle. Principled and focused on achieving worthy goals.

'I'm not the happy ever after you're looking for,' he finally said. 'It's best you accept it from the outset otherwise you'll get hurt in the long run and I would hate that to happen.'

'You don't have the power to hurt me.' Frankie picked up her wine glass and raised it in an airy toast, mentally crossing her fingers in case she was tempting fate. 'To not falling in love.'

Gabriel touched his glass against hers, his eyes holding hers in a steely lock. 'Cheers.'

Once their meal was over, Gabriel them drove back to the villa with his thoughts going back over their dinner conversation. It was a new experience for him to talk about his family with someone. He had not spoken of his mother's death for years. He didn't even talk about it with his sister Carli, mostly because she didn't remember their mother. The phone call out on the terrace earlier that evening had been from one of his brothers. Nothing could sour Gabriel's mood more than a conversation with Ricci. Carli had apparently let slip to Ricci that Gabriel had warned her about associating with the rest of the family. Carli was torn between two worlds—the so-called security of their criminal family and making her own way. So far, she hadn't quite made up her mind.

But somehow, Frankie had got him to open up about his difficult family background—the pain and shame of it he could never quite shake off. He carried it with him like the scar on his face. His past could never be erased no matter how much he tried to distance himself from it. It followed him like a toxic vapour, poisoning his thoughts, robbing him of what little joy he had managed to claw for himself out of living a decent, hardworking and productive life.

Gabriel knew he was flirting with danger by marrying Frankie. She was an old-fashioned girl at heart looking for her handsome prince to ride off into the sunset with her. But he couldn't give her false hope. Neither could he allow her sink into financial ruin while he had the means to protect her. He had calculated the risks, measured them and decided that a short-term marriage would solve both of their problems. Was he a misguided fool for insisting on the no-falling-in-love rule? He'd never had an issue with developing feelings for other partners. He admired and respected many of the women he had dated but he had never developed lasting feelings for any one of them.

But the more time he spent with Frankie the more he realised he had never allowed anyone else close enough to know him. To understand the things that drove him, the ghosts and shadows of his past that had shaped him into who he was today.

When they arrived back at the villa, Gabriel helped Frankie out of the car. She walked with him to the front door and seemed to be as preoccupied as he was. Her smooth forehead was wrinkled in a frown and her teeth kept worrying at her lower lip. 'Tired?' he asked once they were inside the villa.

Her smile was fleeting. 'Not really...'

Before he could stop himself, he took her hand and lifted it to his mouth, pressing his lips against her fingertips. Her pupils flared and her tongue crept out and flicked over the pillowy softness of her cherry-red lips. She lifted her other hand to his face, tracing the scar on his cheekbone with her finger, her touch so light he wondered if he imagined it. But then she stepped up on tiptoe and placed her lips against the scar in a gentle kiss. The soft press of her lips sent a shockwave through his body and it took more willpower than he wanted to admit to stop from pulling her to him and crushing her mouth to his.

But she must have sensed the internal struggle he was enduring. Her gaze met his and her cheeks bloomed with a delicate shade of pink. 'I meant what I said at dinner… Thank you for telling me about your childhood.'

He gave her hand a gentle squeeze and released it. 'I'll see you in the morning. Sleep well.'

Her expression faltered, she gave a couple of rapid blinks, her eyes falling away from his. 'Goodnight…' Her voice was barely above a whisper.

He had only taken a few steps when her voice stalled him. 'Gabriel?'

He turned to look at her. 'Yes?'

She fidgeted with her engagement and wedding rings on her left hand, her teeth pulling at her lower lip. 'Why did you ask me to have dinner with you four years ago?'

'Why does any man ask a woman to dinner? Because he fancies her.'

A small frown began to pull at her forehead. 'My father didn't…erm…put you up to it?' There was an uncertain quality to her voice.

'No. Why would you think that?'

She shrugged but her frown didn't go away. 'I just wondered if he'd suggested it to you…' She bit her lip again.

Gabriel came back to her and tipped up her chin with his finger to lock his gaze with hers. 'Your father had nothing to do with my decision to ask you out. Do you really find it so hard to believe I wasn't attracted to you? Am *still* attracted to you?'

Her eyes were luminous grey-blue pools, shimmering in a whirlpool of doubt and hope. She moved closer as if pulled by the force of a magnet, her hands sliding upwards to rest against his chest, her lower body brushing his. Heating, tempting, torturing him. She lifted her hand to his face, tracing the contour of his mouth, her touch so electrifying his lips fizzed and buzzed and burned.

'Gabriel…' Her voice was barely a thread of sound and yet it resounded with the same need he could feel pummelling his body.

He cupped her face, holding her gaze. 'Tell me what you want, *cara*.'

She moistened her mouth, the flick of her tongue sending a lightning rod of lust to his groin. 'I want you.' She moved closer, pressing her body against the throbbing ache of his. 'Ever since you kissed me earlier today… I just can't stop this ache. Do you…do you feel it too?'

Gabriel wrapped his arms around her curvaceous body, his blood going at rocket speed. 'Can't you feel what you're doing to me?'

Her creamy cheeks became tinged with pink. 'Make love to me?' Her soft tone was touchingly tentative, as if even with the hard evidence of his need pressing against her body, she still couldn't quite believe he wanted her.

Gabriel lowered his mouth to hers, brushing her lips once, twice, three times. 'Are you sure about this? It's been a rollercoaster of a day and you might regret this in the morn—'

She placed her finger over his lips, blocking his speech. 'I won't regret it. I want you. It makes sense to make ours a proper marriage even if it's only for a year.'

He stroked his thumb across the plump softness of her lower lip. 'Let's take this upstairs. I don't fancy making love to you for the first time in the foyer.'

He took her by the hand and led her upstairs, stopping outside his bedroom. He was torn between making passionate love with her and giving her more time to make sure it was what she truly wanted. How could he be sure she didn't feel obliged? He had done all he could to give her the freedom of choosing. He had promised her he would remain faithful even if they didn't consummate their marriage. 'It's not too late to change your mind.'

She glanced at his mouth, her throat rising and falling. 'I'm not going to change my mind.' Her eyes came back to his. 'It's what I want. What I need.'

Gabriel opened the bedroom door and led her inside and closed the door. He needed it too. He needed her.

Badly.

CHAPTER EIGHT

FRANKIE LOOPED HER arms around his neck, her fingers playing with his hair, her mouth crushed beneath the passionate pressure of his. She had been fighting her attraction to him from the moment he'd proposed marriage. Who was she kidding? She had been fighting this fervent attraction for years. And now they were married she could indulge herself in experiencing his lovemaking. Why shouldn't she? It was what she wanted. It was what he wanted too.

Gabriel's tongue danced with hers, stirring her longing until she was making breathless whimpering sounds, aching to get as close as she possibly could. His hands cupped her bottom, drawing her against his hardness, the proud swell of his flesh making everything that was female in her shudder with delight. The slight graze of his jaw against her face when he changed position was a heady reminder of their essential differences. Male and female. Experience and inexperienced.

Should she tell him she was a virgin? The words assembled on her tongue but she couldn't bring herself to say them. She didn't want him to change his mind about making love with her. She didn't want to confirm to him how different she was from his other lovers.

Gabriel groaned against her mouth, one of his hands moving from her bottom to gently cup her breast. His touch, even through the layers of her clothes, was electrifying, thrilling to her senses. 'You are so damn beautiful but you are wearing too many clothes.' His voice was rough with desire, rough and sexy, and it made her legs feel weak to think he was as turned on by her as she was him.

'So are you.'

He shrugged off his jacket and tore the tie from around his neck and tossed it aside, his smouldering eyes holding hers.

Frankie pulled his shirt out of the waistband of his trousers and placed her hands on the warm hard flesh of his back. He undid the buttons and hauled it over his head and threw it in the same direction as his jacket and tie. He slid the zip at the back of her satin dress down and it fell away from her and pooled in a silky puddle at her feet. She wondered why she wasn't feeling shy standing in front of him in just bra and knickers. She felt feminine and sexy, especially with the way his eyes were drinking her curves in. His hands skated over her lace-covered breasts, teasing them with his light touch, sending delicious frissons through her.

His hands came to the edge of her knickers, the touch of his fingers against her belly making her skin tingle and tighten. She sucked in a shuddery breath and he stalled his movements. 'Am I going too fast for you?' His voice had a note of concern, his gaze searching.

Frankie disguised a swallow, her heart racing, her body aching for more of his touch. 'You're not going fast enough.' She went to work on the fastening of his trousers, her fingers brushing over the sprinkling of black hair of his rock-hard abdomen that disappeared in a trail below his waistband.

His hands came to her aid and he unzipped himself, kicking off his shoes, and stepping out of his trousers. Frankie couldn't take her eyes off his body. His gloriously male body—tight and toned and tanned—and the temptation of his hard length beneath his dark blue underwear. She stood on one leg to undo the straps of her stilettoes but almost overbalanced.

'Here. Let me help you.' He bent down in front of her and undid the right shoe and then the left, the skin-on-skin touch making her breath catch.

He straightened and placed his hands on her hips, holding her against the jut of his erection. She moved against him instinctively, searching for his possession as if she had done this many times before. It felt so *right* to be this close. Close enough to feel the throb and pulse of his blood. To feel the heat and potency of his male flesh against the throb and ache of hers.

His mouth came down again, sealing hers in a slow, drugging kiss that made every hair on her scalp tingle at the roots. His tongue played tag with hers, the erotic movements making her lower body burn with damp heat. Her inner core pulsated with the need to feel him inside her, her tender flesh swollen, ready for his possession. His mouth left hers and blazed a hot trail of barely there kisses over her neck and décolletage, every light touchdown of his lips making her almost dizzy with desire.

Frankie slid her hands up to his hair, her fingers playing with the thick dark strands, tugging and releasing, delighting in the sounds of approval he was making when she pressed herself as close as she could. 'I want you. All of you.' Her voice was practically vibrating with desire.

Gabriel came back to crush her mouth beneath his in a deep kiss that played havoc with her senses. She was literally going to *die* if he didn't assuage this searing ache in her flesh. He lifted his head after a moment and his gaze smouldered. 'I want you so badly it's killing me.' His tone was as ragged as his breathing and it made her feel powerfully feminine to have done this to him. Made him breathless with desperate longing.

Frankie pulled down her bra straps off her shoulders, suddenly too shy to take her bra off by herself. He reached behind her and unclipped it, his eyes flaring with heat when they devoured her curves. His hands came around to cup her naked breasts, his touch sending shivers darting down her spine. 'You are beyond beautiful.' His thumbs passed over her sensitive nipples, back and forth, teasing them into even tighter buds. 'So damn gorgeous I can't keep my hands off you.'

'I want your hands on me.' Frankie arched her spine under the lazy rolling of his thumbs, every nerve quivering with pleasure, pleasure that was shooting down in a hot current between her legs.

He brought his mouth to her right breast, kissing the upper curve in a series of light touchdown kisses, teasing her into a stupor of mind-blowing desire. He opened his mouth over her nipple, his tongue circling, tasting, teasing and then his teeth lightly grazed her, making her snatch in a breath. He licked and stroked her breasts in turn, his hands against her ribcage, thankfully holding her upright for she was sure she would have melted into a pool at his feet if he hadn't.

He led her to the bed and peeled away his underwear, hooking a finger in her lace knickers, sliding them down, down, down. Frankie stepped out of them and pressed her body against him, desperate to feel him from her breasts to her thighs.

'Oh, God, I need you…' Her voice came out as an urgent plea.

'I need you too. So damn much.' Gabriel eased her down on the bed and left her briefly to source a condom from his wallet in the back pocket of his jeans. Frankie was shocked that she hadn't once thought of protection as she was so caught up in the heat of the moment. He came back and she couldn't tear her eyes away from his gloriously aroused body. His abdomen was ridged with tight coils of muscle and a line of masculine dark hair that bloomed around his jutting manhood.

He came down beside her, his hand resting on her belly so close to where she ached the most. His eyes roved over her body, his pupils wide and dark with desire. He lowered his head to her belly, his tongue gliding over her skin in a teasing caress that made her back arch like a cat being stroked. Frankie gasped when he separated her feminine folds with his tongue and she shrank away, tense and worried in case she wasn't what he expected.

He settled her with a hand on the curve of her hip. 'Too much, *cara*? Tell me what works for you.'

Hmm… What worked for her was a furtive fumble in the dark with her own fingers on the odd occasion when she felt the need. But there was no way she was going to tell him that. Frankie could feel her cheeks giving enough heat to solve the energy crisis of a small nation. 'I just want you inside me…' It was the truth after all. The other things could wait if she ever worked up the courage to allow him to pleasure her that way.

He cupped her womanhood with a gentle hand. 'Are you sure?'

She took his hand and placed it on her right breast. 'Make love to me. Please?' Okay, so now she was begging but she was beyond caring. She was desperate. Desperate and wanton.

His slow smile made something in her belly do a flip-turn. 'With pleasure.' He sat up to roll on the condom, coming back to her to stroke her from breast to thigh.

Frankie caressed his back and shoulders, urging him with restless movements of her pelvis. He moved over her, resting his weight on his arms, taking care not to crush her, his thighs positioned with hers in a sexy tangle. He nudged her entrance and then groaned and surged forward as if propelled by a force out of his control. Frankie gasped out loud, shocked at the sharp stab of pain as her tender muscles tried to accommodate him.

Gabriel jerked away with a horrified expression. 'Did I hurt you?'

Frankie bit her lip, unable to meet his gaze. 'Erm, not really…'

He tipped up her chin to meet her gaze, shock and dread reflected in his. 'I thought you were ready. Was I rushing you? I'm so sorry I didn't—'

'You weren't rushing me…' *Oh, God, did she have to spell it out?*

A silence stretched like an unexpected pause in a live musical performance.

'Dio mio…' Gabriel's face paled, his mouth opening and closing, his throat rising and falling. 'You were a…a *virgin*?' He leapt off the bed as if she was carrying a deadly virus. He disposed of the condom, his eyes squeezing shut for a moment as if he hoped to open them again and find the last few minutes hadn't happened.

Frankie sat up and wrapped her arms around her bent knees, suddenly embarrassed to be so naked and exposed. 'You don't have to make it sound like it's a fatal disease.'

He scraped a hand through his hair so roughly she heard it from across the room. 'Why on earth didn't you tell me? Why?' His voice was harsh, raw with emotion, his expression still white-tipped with tension. With guilt. 'I hurt you.'

Frankie was close to tears and did everything she could to stop from giving in to them. Her throat closed over with tightness, her chest feeling like it was crushed under a chest of drawers. 'I was embarrassed, that's why.'

A frown pleated his forehead. 'What is there to be embarrassed about?'

She rolled her eyes and pulled the bedcover over her nakedness. 'I'm twenty-five years old, that's

what. Most girls lose their virginity in their teens.
Go me for waiting another decade.'

'Is there a reason you waited this long?' His tone
softened, his expression losing some of its tautness.

'Not really…' She lowered her gaze. 'Well,
maybe…'

Gabriel picked up his trousers and stepped back
into them. The sound of his zip coming back up
ripped through the silence. He came and sat on
the edge of the bed and took one of her hands in
a gentle hold. 'Do you feel comfortable talking
about it?'

Frankie drew in a long breath and slowly released it. 'I was flirting with his guy when I was
sixteen. I had a crush on him. A huge crush. We
started dating but I overheard him telling a friend
he was only dating me so he could crow about it
later. I was a trophy to collect. Nothing more than
a notch he wanted on his bedpost. I basically never
dated again after that humiliation.'

Gabriel caressed her hand in tender strokes.
'I'm sorry that happened to you. Some guys can
be complete and utter jerks.' His fingers gently
squeezed hers. 'But now I feel like a jerk for hurting you. I would never have touched you if—'

'But that's one of the reasons I didn't tell you,'
Frankie said. 'I was worried you wouldn't want
to make love to me for being such a pariah. A pa-
thetic misfit.'

He placed his other hand on her shoulder. 'No, *cara*. Don't say such things.' His voice was deep and rough around the edges. 'Yes, I would've thought twice. Of course I would. But it agonises me to know I've hurt you. I feel deeply ashamed. If I could replay the last few minutes and do things differently I would.'

Frankie turned her hand over in his, meeting his gaze. 'We could press replay…couldn't we?'

He let out a sigh and his hands fell away from her. The wall had come back up. 'We'll go back to keeping our relationship platonic. It's for the best.'

'Platonic?' Frankie coughed out the word. 'Are you serious? Am I that useless in bed that you can't bear to touch me?' Her chin quivered and she sank her teeth into her lip.

He let out a softly uttered curse and came back to sit next to her, taking her hands in his. 'Oh, Frankie. What am I going to do with you?' He pressed a light kiss to the middle of her forehead, his lips on her skin as light as air.

She met his gaze with tears shimmering in her own. 'You called me Frankie…'

He gave a lopsided smile and brushed a strand of hair away from her face. 'I did, didn't I?' His gaze went to her mouth and he drew in a shuddering breath and brought his eyes back to hers. 'Listen to me, *cara*. This can't happen between us. Not now. Not ever. It wouldn't be right on my part to—'

'But you said at the beginning it was up to me if our marriage was a proper one or not.' Frankie clutched at his hand, close to begging. 'You said you would be happy to oblige me. Weren't those your exact words?'

A dull flush rose along his cheekbones and a flicker of pain flashed like a struck match in his gaze. He removed her hand and rose from the bed, his hands going by his sides, clutched in fists as if he was fighting an internal battle not to reach for her. 'Please don't remind me how I spoke to you back then. I assumed you were experienced. That's the only excuse I have for my behaviour.'

'It's not exactly something I felt I should broadcast.' Frankie gave him a baleful look. 'Hey, everybody. Guess what? I'm a flipping virgin at the ripe old age of twenty-five. How do you think that would go down?'

Gabriel dragged his hand down his face, the rasping sound of his stubble against his palm loud in the silence. 'I'm sorry. But I don't think it would be right to take this any further. Today has been a big day, an unusual day, and it's coloured your judgement. You'll see I'm right in the morning.'

Frankie got off the bed, taking the bedcovers with her, throwing him another glance. 'We're going on our honeymoon in the morning. Or have you changed your mind about that too?'

He drew in a breath and released it in a gust.

'No. We'll go as planned to Marseille. The change of scene will do both of us good.' He gave her one of his formal nods and left the room, closing the door with a firm resounding click.

Frankie sat back down on the bed, her shoulders slumping on a sigh. Some honeymoon it was going to be...

Gabriel took a drink out to the terrace. He couldn't bear to be in the villa in case his resolve slipped. There was a war going on inside him. A war between the good man he believed himself to be and the dark part of him that wanted to throw caution to the winds and march back upstairs and make passionate love to Frankie.

But how could he now he knew she was a virgin? He felt sick at the thought of how he had hurt her. He had been so deeply shocked it had rendered him practically speechless. It had felt like someone had hit him with a plank. He had caused her pain. He, who had always prided himself on not being *that* sort of man. He was disgusted with himself that he hadn't been more sensitive, that he hadn't made her comfortable enough to tell him.

It was another reminder of the different worlds they came from—her purity and innocence sullied, stained by his darkness. It was only right that he keep his hands off her now. Right and honourable. She had been keeping herself for someone.

The someone who would marry her and give her what she wanted. What she deserved.

A future. A family. For ever.

He felt ashamed for not realising earlier. It all made perfect sense now in hindsight. The press had never reported anything about her love life. Her father had never mentioned a boyfriend. Frankie was known as an ice princess, cool and poised and classy, but that was because she'd been hurt. Shamed by a jerk of a guy who didn't know how to treat a woman with respect.

But was *he* any better?

He had offered her a short-term marriage. He had given her the choice to make it normal or not. He'd tried to be fair. He'd spent a fortune on saving her from financial ruin. But had it been good-will or greed? Greed for her. Greedy hunger for her delectable body.

And now, with some sort of weird and twisted irony, he had to resist that gorgeous body. He had to resist the temptation of making love to his bride.

On their honeymoon, no less.

CHAPTER NINE

GABRIEL BARELY SPOKE on the way to the airport in Milan from Lake Como other than to exchange a few polite pleasantries. He seemed disinclined to engage in conversation. And when he helped her into the car, it was as if he couldn't bear to touch her, even by accident. His frown threatened to carve his forehead in two and his mouth was set in a grim line, a muscle in his jaw tensing on and off as if he was grinding his molars to powder.

But after a while she could bear his taciturnity no longer. 'Are you still angry with me?'

'Not at you, *cara*.' His hands gripped the steering wheel so tightly his tendons bulged and whitened. 'I'm angry at myself. I can't tell you how angry. I hurt you.' He glanced at her. 'Are you okay? I'm sorry. I should've asked well before now.'

'I'm fine, perfectly fine. But you mustn't blame yourself. I could've told you.' She chewed at her lip and looked down at her hands in her lap. 'I probably should've now that I think about it...'

He reached for her nearest hand and gave it a quick squeeze. 'No. This is not your fault.' His voice was not much more than a rasp of sound. 'I can never forgive myself for hurting you like that. I shouldn't have assumed anything about you.'

'We've both assumed things about each other,' Frankie said, thinking of how many times she had misjudged him.

'I had already released the press announcement before we…before we went to dinner last night.' There was a note of regret in his tone. 'The press will probably be waiting for us at the airport. I can deal with them if you'd rather not say anything.'

'Don't you trust me to say the right thing to them about us?'

'I wouldn't blame you if you didn't.' His expression was as grim as a gravedigger's.

Frankie gave a soft laugh. 'Seriously, Gabriel. You need to lighten up. It's the twenty-first century, you know. Anyone would think you'd committed a heinous crime.'

There was a beat or two of silence.

'I'm sorry. I didn't mean to—' she began.

'It's fine.' His tone was curt, the fleeting movement of his lips nowhere near a smile.

He was right about the press. They were gathered in a group near the departure gate, phones and cameras at the ready.

'Signor Salvetti, the news of your marriage to

Francesca Mancini has stunned everyone. Tell us about your relationship,' one female journalist said.

Gabriel had his arm around Frankie's waist and drew her closer to his side. 'We have been friends for some years. We fell in love recently and decided to marry in private, out of respect for Francesca's recent loss of her father.'

'Francesca, can you tell us how he proposed?' another female journalist asked.

'Erm… He was very romantic but that's all I am going to say,' Frankie said, choosing her words carefully. 'It was a private moment between us that is only our business.'

The journalist wasn't giving up that easily. She swung her recording device in Gabriel's direction. 'Have you introduced your new bride to your father?'

Frankie could feel Gabriel flinch as if someone had struck him. Her heart ached for him having to deal with such a question, knowing now how he felt about his father. 'No. I have nothing to do with my father. I haven't spoken to him in years. Now, if you'll excuse us—we have a plane to catch for our honeymoon.' He led Frankie into the departure hall with firm, *don't-mess-with-me* strides.

And, thankfully, the press got the message and moved on.

'I think we should have rehearsed for that a bit

better back there…' Frankie said once they were on the flight with a drink in front of them.

Gabriel's unreadable gaze met hers. 'I thought you handled it brilliantly. Saying something to them without really saying anything.'

'I didn't want to make something up on the spot that wouldn't be true to your character, I mean, you don't strike me as the romantic type.' She wasn't sure she was being entirely fair but the words were out before she could think twice.

One side of his mouth came up in a wry smile. 'Then it's just as well I'm not intending to woo and win anyone once we end our arrangement. According to you, I'd fail miserably.'

Frankie wasn't sure what to make of his expression. There was a mercurial light in his dark gaze. She sighed and picked up her mineral water. 'I didn't mean to insult you.'

He lifted his finger to her face and sent it down her cheek in a lazy stroke. 'I have thick skin. You should know that about me by now.'

She shivered under his light touch, her gaze going to his mouth as if pulled by invisible strings. 'I wonder if it's as thick and unfeeling as you make out.'

His gaze lingered on her mouth, his finger tracing it in one continual movement that made something in her belly flap and flutter. 'You'd better believe it, *cara*.' His tone had a hint of sadness.

His hand fell away and he turned away to pick up his own drink, a thoughtful frown settling between his brows.

Thankfully, there were no press to greet them in Marseille. Frankie followed Gabriel out to the car he had organised for them complete with chauffeur. They drove through the lively grit and grandeur of France's second largest city. Marseille had a pedigree that stretched back to classical Greece and was a thriving multicultural port and tourist destination, especially after the year it claimed the title of European Capital of Culture. The driver took them to a stunning villa in Bouches-du-Rhône, high up in the prestigious district of Le Roucas-Blanc. The late-nineteenth-century three-storey villa was set facing the sea and the islands beyond. The *calanques*—the steep-sided valleys formed in limestone, dolomite or other carbonate strata—were a spectacular feature of this part of the Mediterranean coast. And the villa, situated with such an amazing outlook, was a perfectly secluded paradise away from the bustling busyness of the tourist-heavy city of Marseille. There were several terraces, each with a garden, and one even had an infinity pool, and Frankie couldn't wait to explore everything.

'Oh, my goodness, it's amazing…' She swung her gaze back to Gabriel. 'What a gorgeous place.'

'I'm glad you like it.' He gave one of his fleeting smiles. 'I bought it a year or so ago after waiting for it for a decade. The previous owners didn't want to sell but then I finally managed to convince them. I've only just finished having it redecorated.'

Frankie's eyes widened to the size of saucers. Satellite saucers. 'You *own* it?'

'*Sì.* I like it here. It's private.'

She had grown up with wealth and privilege but this villa was something else again. She had been to Marseille once before with her father and a school friend and stayed in a luxury hotel. But she couldn't help thinking the privacy and seclusion of this villa couldn't have been a more perfect place for a honeymoon. *If she were indeed having a honeymoon.*

But how like him to wait for something he wanted. He set a goal and had the patience and self-discipline to finally achieve it. In a world of immediate gratification, of snatch and grab and don't measure the risks first, how could she not admire him?

How could she not fall a *little* bit in love with him?

The driver deposited their luggage inside and left soon after.

Frankie followed Gabriel into the villa where fresh flowers were arranged in crystal vases in the foyer. There was a tasteful blend of old and new in the choice of colours and furnishings. There was a grand staircase leading to the other floors but no sign of any staff.

Gabriel took her upstairs to the suite he'd allocated her. She couldn't help thinking he was treating her like a house guest instead of a bride. His bedroom was as far away from hers as it could be.

'Do you have staff here?' Frankie asked.

'I have a small team of people who take care of things,' Gabriel said, putting her bag down on a low-lying chest that serviced as a luggage rack. 'Gardeners and a housekeeper. She only comes in a couple of times a week when I'm here. I don't like being surrounded by staff when I come here to get away from everyone.'

'I hope my presence won't play havoc with your much-prized solitude?'

He grazed her cheek with the back of his knuckles, an inscrutable smile pulling at the edges of his mouth. 'You play havoc with much more than my solitude, *cara*. Much more.'

She looked into his dark as night gaze, her breath stalling in her throat. She lifted her hand to his face, tracing the scar on his cheekbone. 'Why are you so determined to push me away?'

He drew in a breath and placed his hands on her shoulders. 'You know why.' His voice had that deep burr that sent a tremor down her spine and a shockwave through her core.

'But I want you close.' Frankie moved so she was touching him from chest to thigh. 'Can't you see that?'

His fingers tightened momentarily on her shoulders, a battle playing out on his face. His jaw worked, his eyes darkened, his mouth flattened. 'If I were a good man I would walk out of this room and not look back.'

'But?' Frankie's eyes searched his, her heart thudding so hard it felt like it was going to punch through the wall of her chest like a fist through damp paper.

He sighed again and cupped her cheek. 'Seems I'm not the decent man I thought I was.' His mouth came down and pressed a gentle kiss to her lips. It was brief but no less magical. Her lips sang under the light press of his, aching for more. He raised his mouth just a fraction above hers. 'Tell me to get out of here before it's too late.'

Frankie slid her hand along the side of his stubbly jaw, her mouth so close to his, their breaths mingled. 'I want you to make love to me. I want it more than anything. Please?'

He drew in a ragged breath, his hands taking her again by the shoulders. At first, she thought he was going to put her away from him, but she saw the exact moment when his resolve weakened. His features lost their lines of tension, muscle by muscle. 'As long as we both know this is just sex.

It's not a future together. It's just an affair for the length of our marriage.'

'I understand.' Frankie pressed closer, her hands linking around his neck. 'This is all I want. I can't bear to get any older without some experience. And who better than you to give it to me?'

'You make it so damn hard to resist you.' His cupped her bottom, drawing her closer to the hard heat of his body. 'Are you sure about this? Really sure?'

She pulled his head down so his mouth was just above hers. 'I'm sure.'

His mouth covered hers in a scorching kiss, a deep groan sounding at the back of his throat when she opened to him. His tongue tangoed with hers, leading it in a sensual dance that made every bone in her body melt until she was only standing upright because he was holding her. She thought for a moment the floor was shifting beneath her feet, but then she realised he had picked her up and was carrying her to his bedroom further down the hall. He stopped to kiss her on the way, time and time again, so that when they finally arrived in his room, she was mad with the need to touch him skin on skin.

He lowered her to the floor, sliding her down the length of his body, his eyes glittering with desire. 'I need to take things slowly. I don't want to hurt you.'

Frankie set to work on his clothes, her fingers fumbling in her haste, terrified he might be having second thoughts about making love to her. 'I want to touch you.'

He placed a hand over hers, holding it against his chest where his heart was beating like someone in an emergency cardiac unit. 'It's important to me that you enjoy this every step of the way.' He lowered his mouth back to hers in a long bone-melting kiss, his tongue playing with hers in languorous strokes that made her senses spin. He peeled the clothes from her body, his touch gentle and careful as if he was unwrapping something infinitely precious.

His hands caressed her breasts through the lace of her bra before he unclipped it and let it fall to the floor. He stepped back and removed the rest of his clothes, leaving her in just her knickers. She couldn't take her eyes off his body. The ridges and planes of hard male muscle that so excited her.

She stroked her hand down from his sternum to just above his erection. 'Can I touch you?' Her voice was little more than a whisper.

He groaned and anchored her hand under his against his surging body. 'I've been dreaming of this.' He sucked in a breath and she encircled him with her fingers, going on instinct, caressing him, stroking and massaging him until he was so full and tight she thought he would explode.

After a moment, he pushed her hand away. 'This time is about you. Only you.' He hooked a finger in her knickers and lowered them down her thigh. She stepped out of them, shocked at how sensual the lace felt moving down her leg. Shocked and thrilled by the electric heat of his hand moving along her thigh. Would there ever be a time when his touch wouldn't thrill her so much? Would a year be long enough to satiate the desire he had awakened?

Gabriel led her to the king-sized bed, pausing to take a condom from the bedside drawer. Had he brought other women here? The thought was as unwelcome as a deadly spider on the crisp white sheets. She hadn't realised she'd made a sound until he glanced at her with a narrowed gaze. 'Is something wrong?'

Frankie sank her teeth into her lip and aimed her gaze at the shallow dish at the base of his neck between his collar bones. 'Nothing…'

He brought her chin up so she couldn't avoid his gaze. He searched her gaze for a long moment. 'I haven't brought anyone else here before you.'

'No one?'

'No one.' His finger brushed over her bottom lip in a barely touching movement.

'But why not?'

'The redecorating for one thing.' He dropped his hand from her face and let out a sigh. 'And the other thing…' A frown played on his forehead. 'I'm not sure. I only ever planned to come here alone.'

Frankie didn't want to think about why his words pleased her so much. She didn't want to set herself up for future pain by dreaming for something more than he was offering. She had made the decision to marry him on his terms. It would be foolish of her to hanker after a happy ending he was incapable or unwilling to give. Wasn't it enough that he wanted her? Wanted her fervently if his body was any indication? She moved closer, touching his lean jaw with her fingers. 'I'm glad that I don't have to compete with any other memories you've had in this bed.'

'We can make our own memories, *si*?' He encircled her wrist with his fingers, turning her hand over and kissing her palm and then all the way up her arm until he was close to her naked breast. His mouth brushed her skin, teasing every pore into a frenzy. It was both pleasure and torture, a tantalising caress that made her ache for more. His lips moved along the curve of her breast, his tongue circling her nipple, his teeth taking it between them in a soft bite that sent a ripple of pleasure to her core. He did the same to her other breast, making her nipple tighten into a pert bud, making her desire for him quake through her body in pulsing waves and flickers.

He lay on the bed with her, his hand stroking her from her breasts to her belly, long lazy strokes that made her flesh tingle. He brought his head down to her stomach, circling her bellybutton with his tongue before going lower. She drew in a breath and tensed but he calmed her with a gentle hand, just above her mound.

'Relax for me, *cara*. I want to make it good for you.'

Frankie lay back and gave herself up to the sensation of him exploring her intimate folds. The movement of his lips, the stroke and glide of his tongue against her swollen flesh sent ripples and shockwaves through her. And then, almost without warning, her body erupted in a tumult of feeling. Darts and arrows, waves and shudders of pleasure rocketed through her lower body, travelling through her thighs and pelvis like liquid fire. She gasped and writhed under his expert touch, her body so out of her control it was almost frightening.

She flung herself back against the pillows with a breathless sigh, stunned that her body could have reacted in such a powerful way. 'I had no idea…' She could barely get the words out. Her heart was still hammering as if she had just run up to the top of a lighthouse.

Gabriel stroked the hair back from her face, planting a light kiss on her mouth. She could taste herself on him, the musk of female arousal and response. And rather than make her shy and uncomfortable, it made her feel close to him in a way she had never expected to feel. 'You were magnificent,' he said. 'Truly magnificent.'

Frankie stroked her hand down his chest to the flat plane of his abdomen. 'But what about you?'

'We'll get to that…' He brought his mouth back to hers, kissing her with such exquisite thoroughness her desire built back up again in a fiery rush. He moved his mouth to send a hot trail of kisses over her breasts, down her stomach and back up again.

'I want you…' Frankie was close to begging, her arms pulling him closer, her lower body arching up to meet his.

He put on a condom and came back to her, his body arranged over hers without allowing her to bear too much of his weight. The feel of his hair-roughened thighs entwined with her smooth ones made her shiver with excitement. The hardness of his body, so close to the aching swollen heat of hers, made her desperate to have him closer. As close as a man and woman could be.

'I want to take this really slowly.' His tone was as gentle as his hand resting on the flank of her thigh. As gentle as his concerned gaze. 'Tell me if you're not comfortable.'

'Okay…' She was barely capable of speech with her desire for him rampaging through her body.

He positioned himself at her entrance, slowly parting her folds, moving inch by inch, stopping to gauge her reaction. 'Okay so far?'

'More than okay.' She grasped him by his toned and taut buttocks and drew him even closer. The smooth glide of his body within hers took her breath away.

He stilled at the sound of her slight gasp. 'Too much?'

Frankie arched her pelvis to take more of him in. 'Too little.'

A smouldering light burned in his sexily hooded gaze. 'Let's see what I can do about that.'

He went deeper, his thrusts slow and measured, her body welcoming him, worshipping his thick male presence. Shudders and quivers rippled through her body, tension building like a storm about to erupt. His breathing became just as hectic as hers, the movements of his hips increasing in pace, driven by primal lust that craved only one end.

Frankie was with him all the way, her body reacting, responding, relishing the sensations he was delivering in each and every powerful thrust. The tension rose in her core, an unbearable, frantic tension that pleaded for release. Now. Now. Now. She was close but not close enough, the friction of his body against hers teasing her, torturing her. 'I don't think I can—' she gasped out in desperation.

'Yes, you can. I'll help you.' He brought his hand down between their bodies, caressing her swollen flesh, the stroke and flicker of his fingers triggering a cataclysmic release that was like an earthquake through her body. Tumultuous waves rolled and thrashed and crashed through every inch of her flesh. Prickles and tingles and shivers of delight coursed through her from the top of her scalp to her curling toes.

Frankie was still trying to get her breathing under control when he tensed all over, his own release powering through him. He gave a shuddering groan and with those final, desperate thrusts spilled his essence. She stroked her hands over the goose-bumps peppering his back and shoulders, her body still reeling from the sensations it had experienced.

Gabriel moved away slightly to dispose of the condom, and then came back and leaned on one elbow to look at her, his eyes as dark as black holes in space. He moved his hand from the curve of her waist to her hip and back again in long lazy strokes that made her flesh tingle. 'You were amazing.' His voice was low and deep.

'No. You were.' Frankie threaded her fingers through the thickness of his hair. 'Thank you.'

A flicker of something came and went in his

gaze as quick as a camera shutter click. 'I didn't hurt you?'

'Not at all.' She moved her hand to his face, stroking her index finger down from the bridge of his nose to the bottom of his chin. 'Was it good for you too? I mean...*really* good?' She couldn't quite meet his gaze.

He cupped one side of her face, locking her gaze with his. 'It was amazing. *You* were amazing.' He waited a beat and added, 'No regrets?'

'No. You?'

Desire glittered and shimmered in his gaze. 'Not yet.' And his mouth came back down to hers.

CHAPTER TEN

GABRIEL LEFT FRANKIE to have a nap and went downstairs to the kitchen to get a glass of water. The glass of water he could just have easily got from the en suite, but he was forcing himself to stay away in case he was tempted to make love to her yet again. He was conscious of her inexperience and didn't want to make her sore. He had expected the chemistry between them to be powerful, but not *that* powerful. More powerful than any other sexual encounter he had ever had. His body was still humming with the aftershocks, his skin tingling from her touch, the taste of her sweet in his mouth.

Her response to him thrilled him in a way he hadn't thought possible. He didn't like acknowledging it, but sex had become a little pedestrian for him lately. It was a physical need he satisfied with short, no-strings encounters. He couldn't remember the last time he had lain beside someone and played with their hair while they slept. He couldn't remember wanting someone so badly. He couldn't remember feeling a connection before that went beyond the pleasurable physical union of bodies.

Something about Frankie was different. Unique. Special. Not just her lack of experience—although he'd be lying if he said he hadn't felt honoured and privileged she had wanted him to be her first. He was a fully signed up member of the No Double Standards Club, but even so, the thought that, no matter what happened between them in the future, he would always remain her first lover was intensely delightful.

Gabriel turned on the tap and filled a glass and drank it in a couple of swallows. He could have spent the rest of the evening in that bed with Frankie. The rest of the month. The rest of the year…which was a timely reminder their relationship was only temporary.

One year and one year only.

He had laid down the rules and she had agreed to them. She said she had no regrets, but how soon before she did? Had he made a mistake by making love to her? But how could he call the amazing sex they'd shared a mistake?

No. It was a mistake not to make the most of their time together. They both knew the rules and he had no problem sticking to them.

The only question being…would Frankie?

* * *

Frankie hadn't realised she had drifted off to sleep until she woke to the sound of Gabriel's phone ringing on the bedside table. She sat up but there was no sign of him. She glanced at the phone and her chest gave a tight spasm when she saw a woman's name come up on the screen. Who on earth was Carli? One of his past lovers? A current lover he had put on pause while he was married to Frankie? She was tempted to answer the phone to find out but before she could reach out her hand, Gabriel came striding into the room.

He came over to the bed and snatched up the phone. 'Sorry. I forgot I left it here.' He turned to one side and answered it. 'Can you hold for a second?' he said to the person on the line in Italian, and then gestured to Frankie that he had to take the call. He turned and walked out of the room, closing the door like he was putting up a barrier.

Jealousy spiked in her like a thousand poisonous arrows, piercing her self-esteem as if it were little more than a child's party balloon. But wasn't that what she was? A child, for thinking Gabriel would not have his bit on the side? He was a man of the world, a playboy who exchanged lovers as easily as changing his shirt.

Frankie got off the bed and dressed, not caring that her clothes were crumpled and creased. She couldn't bear to look herself in the mirror. She didn't want any reminders of how foolish she had been to make love with Gabriel. How foolish she had been to think she was someone special, someone he actually cared about instead of yet another sexual conquest.

The rational part of her brain told her the woman called Carli could be a staff member of his, an employee in his business. But if so, why had he felt the need for privacy? The young woman was a pretty darned gorgeous-looking employee, however. Frankie had caught a glimpse of the photo of the woman that flashed up on the screen. A bottle blonde with big eyes and pouty lips.

Why had Frankie allowed herself to be humiliated?

Gabriel had gone to his study on the lower floor to talk to his sister. For once, Carli's call hadn't been a distressed one but he hadn't wanted to take any chances in front of Frankie. He wasn't used to having an audience when he dealt with yet another of his sister's dramas. His sister had rung to congratulate him—in her inimitable way, that was. Carli wasn't easy to win over, and he worried she might offend or upset Frankie if he allowed them to meet in person.

He couldn't possibly keep his sister a secret from Frankie for an entire year, but neither did he want Carli to get too close to Frankie, because it might complicate things when their marriage came to an end. He didn't want his sister to get too invested in his relationship with Frankie. He didn't want to get too invested either. His plan was for a clean break when the time was up.

It would be fairer for all parties.

He slipped his phone into the back pocket of his jeans and went back upstairs. Frankie was dressed in her travelling clothes and standing in front of the windows overlooking the ocean, her back as stiff and unyielding as an ironing board. Was it his imagination or was there a current of tension in the air?

'Frankie? Are you okay?'

She turned, her arms tightly crossed over her chest, her look so cold she could have snap-frozen him on the spot. 'I hate to sound like a jealous wife, but who the hell is Carli?' Her voice was strained as if she was holding back a torrent of emotions.

'She's my sister.'

Her mouth opened and closed, her eyes widening in surprise. 'Your…your *sister*? You didn't say anything about having a sister.'

Gabriel rubbed a hand over his face and sighed. 'Yes, well, I like to keep her out of the public if and when I can.'

Frankie's expression had lost its coldness only to be replaced by puzzlement. 'But I don't understand…' Hurt flashed through her gaze. 'Why didn't you say something to me before now?'

'I'm sorry for not telling you. But I had my reasons.'

Her eyebrows rose in twin arches. 'Which are?'

'Carli is…unwell.'

Concern flickered across Frankie's face. 'Oh, no. What's wrong with her?'

He drew in a long breath and released it. 'She has an eating disorder. I've been trying to help her overcome it but it's a Sisyphean battle. I never know from one day to the next if she's going to be okay.'

She put her hand to her throat in a shocked gesture. 'I'm so sorry. It must be absolute agony for you.'

He sat on the edge of the bed, placing his hands either side of his thighs. 'Yes, it is. But I can't leave her to fend for herself. I have to do whatever I can to limit her contact with my father and brothers. They are not a good influence.'

Frankie came over to the bed and sat beside him, one of her hands coming to rest on top of his thigh. 'I'm so sorry for making such a ridiculous scene just then. I thought…' She bit her lip and continued. 'Never mind what I thought. The important thing is if Carli is okay. Is she?'

Gabriel placed his hand over the top of hers. 'She's fine, for now. She was the reason I didn't get to your father's funeral. I had to stay with her for a bit until I felt she was out of danger. She was calling to congratulate us. I told her the other day we were getting married.'

'Was she…surprised?'

'A little.' He tucked a strand of her hair behind her ear and gave another sigh. 'I didn't tell her all the details about our marriage. It's best she thinks it genuine like everyone else. If she became annoyed with me, she would sell our secret to the press in the blink of an eye.'

Frankie's gaze was troubled. 'I'd like to meet her sometime…that is, if you think she would like to meet me? I wouldn't let slip that we're not really in love or anything.'

Gabriel smoothed away her frown with his thumb. 'I'll see what can be arranged. Carli isn't all that reliable when it comes to keeping appointments.' He lowered his hand from her face and took her hand once more, his fingers absently stroking the back of her hand.

'She's younger than you, yes?'

'By seven years. She's the same age as you— twenty-five—but you wouldn't think it in terms of her behaviour sometimes.'

'It can't have been easy for her growing up without a mother…' Sadness swam in her gaze. 'How old was she when…?'

'Carli was only two years old when our mother died. She was still in nappies.'

'Oh, how terribly sad,' Frankie said. 'Does she remember your mother at all?'

'No. Nothing.' He gave a rueful grimace. 'I wasn't much of a replacement figure but I did what I could.'

'But what about your father? Or other relatives? Aunts or grandparents or—'

'My mother married my father against her family's wishes. She was cast out of their lives and they didn't even come to her funeral. It was as if she had never existed.'

Frankie gripped his hand. 'But how on earth did you manage? You were only a little child yourself.'

'I had no choice,' Gabriel said. 'My father's idea of looking after a small child was to leave her in her cot for hours on end. There wasn't the money back then for a nanny or babysitter. There was barely enough money for food. I missed almost a whole year of school because I didn't want to leave Carli with anyone my father chose to babysit.'

He flattened his mouth and continued. 'He's the reason she's so messed up. He was always shouting at her for crying, but what little kid doesn't cry, even if they hadn't just lost their mother?' His chest ached when he recalled Carli's piteous cries. He had done all he could to comfort her, suppressing his own tears because he hadn't wanted to add to her distress. He had done such a good job of locking away his emotions that these days he struggled to access them when he needed them most.

Tears shone in Frankie's eyes. 'Oh, Gabriel, it's just so awful that you and Carli and your brothers went through such hell. I can't believe how you turned your life around to become what you are today. How did you do it?'

'I was determined to make something of myself, I felt I owed it to my mother. She hadn't had a good education and I know it was one of the reasons she felt so powerless in her marriage. I wanted to honour her memory by taking every opportunity I could to make a decent life for myself and my siblings.' He gave her a twisted effigy of a smile. 'Not that I was successful in achieving that with any of them. Carli is probably the brightest of all four of us and yet she didn't finish high school. It's one of the failures that most tortures me. Her life is turning out like a train wreck and there's nothing I can do to stop it.'

'But you're doing all you can and that's all anyone can ask of you,' Frankie said, her tone touchingly sincere. 'You sound like the most amazing brother. She's so lucky to have you watching out for her. Your mother would be so proud of who you've become. In spite of all the obstacles thrown at you.'

Gabriel gave her thigh a little pat. 'Enough of this dismal talk.' He stood and drew her up from the bed, holding her loosely in the circle of his arms. 'Now, I don't know about you, but I'm starving. Have a shower and get changed for dinner. I've made a booking and I've called the driver to pick us up in an hour.'

About an hour later, Frankie was sitting with Gabriel in a fine dining restaurant in Marseille. They were seated at a table in a quiet corner, the lighting low and intimate, the décor plush and luxurious. She was still mulling over all he had told her about his sister. While it had stung her that he hadn't told her about Carli before, she understood his reasons given his ongoing worries about her. She looked across the table at him as he examined the menu, wondering how she could have misjudged him so badly.

He hadn't come to her father's funeral, not because he didn't want to but because he had been looking after his sister. She had always thought him arrogant and a little closed off, but why wouldn't he be, given the heartache and suffering he had endured from such a young age? He was still suffering it, each day a living nightmare of gut-wrenching worry for his sister.

How could Frankie keep an emotional distance when he had those wonderful qualities? Qualities of love and loyalty and commitment to his sister no matter what. Frankie knew some of what he was up against in trying to help his sister make something of her life. Her work as a special needs teacher had taught her how much a child's background could jeopardise positive educational outcomes.

Gabriel looked up from the menu and caught her surveying him. 'Have you decided what you'd like?'

What Frankie would like was to start their relationship again. To put it on a different footing, a more permanent footing. But she could never say that. It wasn't what he wanted—he had made that unmistakably clear. 'I was thinking the bouillabaisse.'

'Good choice.' He smiled and closed his menu. 'It's a traditional Provencal fish stew that originated at the port of Marseille. But no doubt you knew that, *si*?'

'I did, actually.' She gave a wry smile. 'My boarding school education in London was not entirely a waste of time.' She paused for a beat and continued. 'Speaking of education... I could help your sister if she wanted to complete her schooling. Lots of mature age students do it and—'

'It's a generous offer but I think it best if we limit the contact between you and my sister.' His tone had an undercurrent of intractability.

Frankie frowned. 'But why? Do you think me

incapable of dealing with her? I've dealt with children from difficult backgrounds, children with complex emotional and physical issues and I've—'

'I've engaged tutors for her before and it's been a waste of time and money.' His expression was grim. 'Besides, I don't want her to get too invested in our relationship.'

'Because it's not permanent?'

'Precisely.' The firm set to his mouth and the hardness in his gaze told her the conversation was now closed.

The waiter came to take their order and once he had gone, Frankie sipped her wine in silence. She could understand Gabriel's concern for his sister, especially if Carli developed a close relationship with her. It would be difficult when their marriage came to its inevitable end. But friendships were often maintained post-divorce between relatives of the couple, sometimes even between the couple themselves. Or was Gabriel so determined to eject her from his life once the year was up? Did he expect the end of their marriage would be the end of their friendship? For that was what she was coming to enjoy about their relationship—not just the amazing lovemaking but the sense of having someone to talk to, someone who understood and listened to her. Respected her.

Gabriel reached across the table and took her

hand. 'Don't be angry with me, *cara*. Think of my decision as damage control.'

Frankie pulled her hand away and placed it in her lap. 'Look, I'm not expecting you to introduce me to all your family. But Carli is obviously someone you deeply care about. What if I could help her?'

The marble-hard screen came up in his gaze. 'It won't help her when we divorce.'

'Are you and I to never see or speak to each other again? Is that what you've planned?'

A muscle beat in his jaw. 'A clean break will be better. Less complicated.'

A tight ache spread through her chest, a cruel invisible hand clutching her heart. 'Is that how you end all your other relationships? Goodbye and good luck and thanks for the memories?'

'Works for me.' The cold finality in his voice was as deadly as the drop of a guillotine.

'Well, it doesn't work for me. I can't just dismiss someone from my life like throwing out milk after the use-by date.'

'Francesca, we discussed this at the outset. One year and one year only.' The indomitable note in his tone was a perfect match for the tight set to his mouth.

Frankie picked up her wine and glared at him over the rim of the glass. 'You know what I've noticed about you? You only call me Francesca when you want to put a barrier up.' She took a sip of her wine and put the glass down.

His gaze didn't waver from hers but something moved at the back of it, like the surreptitious movements of a stagehand during a performance. 'I don't want to argue with you.' His tone softened but the tautness of his jaw did not. 'My concern is you'll want more than I can give, especially now that we're sleeping together. Good sex can muddy the waters.'

'But not for you, clearly.' Frankie couldn't take the barb out of her voice. 'You have amazing sex all the time, don't you?'

'It's hardly a crime.' He let out a breath and placed his hand over hers where it was resting on the table. 'I don't want you to think what we shared wasn't special because it was. Very special. I will never forget it.' The warm press of his hand sent a current of electricity through her body, her skin recognising and welcoming his touch. Wanting more of it. Needing it. Craving it, no matter what his terms were.

Frankie gave a twisted smile. 'Nice to know I'm unforgettable.'

He gave her fingers a gentle squeeze. 'You are. Unbelievably so.'

CHAPTER ELEVEN

THE NEXT TEN days were spent exploring the region on day trips, visiting some of the tourist hot spots but often going to more secluded places to get away from the crowds. Gabriel had organised picnics that they shared on quieter beaches where they could see the *calanques* up close. There had been dinners and dancing at nightclubs and several shopping trips where he had bought her outfit after outfit. She only had to look at something and he had it on the counter and paid for with a flash of his credit card.

At some point on most days Gabriel would retreat to his study to work. His phone was a constant companion and she tried not to be irritated by him being distracted by messages and emails. He had a large business to run and he took the responsibility for his employees seriously. He had told her things were more settled with his position on the board now that news had got out about his marriage to her.

It was a good feeling to know she had helped him in some way. She still felt a little conflicted about the amount of money he had spent on rescuing her from financial ruin. Terribly conflicted. But whenever she raised the topic with him, he seemed unwilling to discuss it.

Just like the topic of when the time would be up on their marriage. She had resigned herself to it being a no-go area as she didn't want to spoil their time in France with bickering. She was enjoying being with him too much. Learning more about him, uncovering the deep players of his personality.

Frankie had taken herself out to the heated infinity pool to fill in the time until Gabriel was finished in the study. The sun was surprisingly warm and she couldn't resist doing a few leisurely laps to cool off. The water sparkled like scattered diamonds as she carved her way through it, and she felt a pang of regret that tomorrow they would be heading back to Milan.

Their honeymoon would be over.

Gabriel got up from his desk after completing some pressing paperwork and went to the window that overlooked the terraced gardens. He could see Frankie swimming in the pool below, her beautiful body dressed in a tiny black bikini he had bought for her in Marseille. Personally, he preferred her without clothes. He never got tired of looking at her, touching her, making love to her. Her confidence had grown with him sexually and he delighted in how she responded to him so enthusiastically. He couldn't remember enjoying sex on this level before. Sex had been a physical thing. A bodily need that could be satisfied.

But making love with Frankie took it to a new level, made it less a bodily need and more of an emotional one. And that was what worried him the most. He was allowing her closer than he had allowed anyone. He had shared not just his body, but his background, his heartache, his struggles.

His vulnerability.

There was a nagging worry that his relationship with her was moving into new territory.

Dangerous territory.

Frankie came to the end of the pool and saw Gabriel standing there with a towel slung around his hips and a glinting look in his eyes. She knew that look so well now. The *I-want-to-have-sex-with-you* look. It made her skin tingle and tighten all over. 'Have you got anything on under that towel?' she asked, with a coy smile.

'Why don't you take it off me and see?'

A quiver coursed through her body and she came up the steps to stand in front of him. His gaze ran over her in a smouldering sweep, triggering a throbbing ache between her thighs. She tip-toed her fingers down from the base of his throat to just above the edge of the towel, delighted in the way his breathing changed as if her touch excited him as much as his excited her. She circled his navel with her finger, then whipped off the towel to find him naked and powerfully aroused.

'Well, look what I found.' She stroked him with her hand and he gave a deep groan, his legs bracing for her touch. She bent down in front of him, caressing her with her lips and tongue until he was breathing heavily, the sounds coming from his throat more urgent, more desperate.

'No. Not yet.' His voice was raw and rough with desire and he hauled her up to her feet, grasping her by the hips. 'I have other plans for you.'

He untied her string bikini, letting both pieces drop in wet puddles at their feet. His hands cradled her breasts, his thumbs rolling over the nipples, his gaze as hot as a blazing fire. He put one hand just below her right breast, pushing it up to meet the descent of his mouth. His lips moved over her sensitive flesh, his tongue circling her nipple, licking and stroking until she was sagging at the knees. He subjected her other breast to the same exquisite torture, leaving no inch of her skin unexplored. He took her by the hand and led her to the double sun lounge inside the cabana near the pool.

By the time he came down beside her, Frankie

was desperate with need. She sat astride him, her feminine folds alive with excited tingling nerves. She leaned over him, her damp hair tickling his chest, and joined her mouth with his, opening her lips to welcome the stabbing thrust of his tongue.

He groaned and grasped her by the hips, his arousal hard and thick against her entrance. '*Dio*, I want you so badly.' His voice was a hoarse growl.

She didn't give him time to pull away to find a condom, even if he had thought to bring one with him. She fed him into her with a deft move of her hand and cried out loud as he went in up to the hilt. She rode him with urgent movements, her body responding to the hard friction of his with intense spasms of pleasure.

'I'll pull out before I—' he began.

'You don't need to. I'm on the Pill to help with my cycle.' Frankie couldn't bear for him to interrupt the delicious rhythm of their bodies. Her senses were on fire and her racing blood heating her core into a pool of molten lava.

His hands gripped her by the upper arms, his gaze suddenly piercing. 'You take it regularly?'

'Yes, of course I do.'

Gabriel seemed to hesitate but then Frankie moved on him again and he groaned and restarted his thrusts to meet the downward pressure of her body. She could feel her orgasm approaching, the build-up of tension in her swollen flesh almost like torture. She shifted position slightly and suddenly she was flying free, catapulted into a blissful oblivion where nothing mattered but the storm of release coursing through her body.

Within seconds, he came with a deep, agonised groan, his hands gripping her by the hips almost to the point of pain. Frankie could feel his essence within her body, the sharing of bodily fluids making her wonder if she would ever feel the same intense intimacy with anyone else.

How could she when she couldn't imagine feeling attracted to anyone but him? He played her body like a maestro played a temperamental instrument. He knew every nuance of her response to his touch, could read every contraction or relaxation of her muscles.

Gabriel relaxed his grip on her upper arms, a frown tugging at his forehead when he saw the imprint of his fingerprints on her skin. 'Sorry, *cara*.' He stroked her arms in soft massaging strokes. 'I was being too rough.'

Frankie leaned forward to brush his lips with hers. 'I like it when you're rough. I'm not made of porcelain, you know.'

He pushed her hair back from her face in a tender movement that made something in her stomach swoop. 'You never cease to surprise me.' His eyes contained a light she had never seen in them before. Dark. Devilish. Dangerous. He suddenly turned her over so she was lying beneath him, one of his muscled thighs hooked over hers. 'Now I've got you where I want you.'

Frankie gave herself up to the passionate crush of his mouth, her arms winding around waist, holding him as close as she possibly could. Shivers raced down her spine when his teeth took her lower lip in a playful bite, the gentle tug triggering a shockwave through her flesh. He passed the tip of his tongue over her lip where his teeth had snagged her in a sweeping salve that made the hairs on her scalp tingle at the roots.

He moved from her mouth to her breasts, his teeth softly nipping at the flesh, his tongue following with a healing lick. His caresses were exciting and thrilling and just this side of dangerous. But she wasn't going to let him have all the fun. When his mouth came back to hers, she used her teeth the same way he had on her. Nipping, tugging, playfully teasing him in kittenish bites that made him growl deep in his throat and tighten his hold.

Before she knew it, he had flipped her over onto her stomach, his hair-roughened thighs trapping her. Feverish excitement raced through her from head to foot. She opened her legs for him, arching her spine so he had easy access to where she wanted him the most. He drove into her with a guttural groan and began thrusting with deep, urgent thrusts that made her entire skin lift in a shower of goose-bumps. His breathing was as hectic as hers, the rhythm of his body within her sending fizzing, whizzing fireworks through her blood. The tension in her core was unbearable. Need clawed at her with ravenous jaws. She was whimpering and gasping and almost sobbing with the desire to come.

Gabriel read the need in her body as she knew he would and placed his hand between her trembling legs and tipped her over the edge. She flew into the stratosphere with a high cry of intense rapture, her body quaking and quivering as the rush of sensations swept through her like a tidal wave. He followed with his own release, his thrusts hard and fast and deep, his body tensing in those final moments before he let go. He collapsed over her, his head buried against her neck, his arms splayed either side of her.

Frankie savoured the moment, the stillness and peace after the sensual storm. She breathed in the scent of their lovemaking, the musk and salt and sweat as fragrant as any expensive cologne.

Gabriel rolled off her and turned her in the circle of his arms so they were lying side by side. One of his hands tidied her hair in gentle strokes that were in stark contrast to the frenzied movements only moments before. 'For the first time in my life, I'm going to hate going back to work.' He kissed her on the tip of the nose and smiled. 'I could get used to this. Way too used to it.'

Frankie stroked his lean jaw, gazing into his espresso-dark eyes. 'You work too hard. Do you *ever* turn off your phone?'

He gave a rueful grimace. 'No.'

'Because of your sister? In case she needs you?'

He sighed and turned onto his back, keeping her tucked up against his side. His hand stroked up and down her bare arm in a slow, smooth caress. 'It's one of the reasons I can't bear the thought of having a family of my own.'

For some reason Frankie couldn't quite explain, his confession made her heart contract as if it had been pinched. Hard. Painfully, cruelly hard. She kept her head resting on his chest, not willing to meet his gaze. 'But surely you would provide your children with a much better upbringing than your father did?'

'True. But having been a stand-in parent for my siblings since I was nine, and with all Carli's ongoing dramas, I can safely say I've had more than my fill of parental responsibility.' There was a chord of finality in his tone that was disquieting.

Disquieting and distressing, because she could think of no better father material than Gabriel. He was strong and steady, caring and hard working. Images popped up in her head of him cradling a newborn baby, his large male hands cupping the infant's tiny head with exquisite gentleness and care.

Their newborn baby.

The baby she could not imagine having with anyone else.

A lengthy silence ticked past.

Frankie stroked her hand over his toned pectoral muscles, then circled his flat male nipple with her finger. 'You never know…one day you might change your mind.'

Gabriel turned his head to look at her, a frown pleating his forehead. 'Don't get any crazy ideas, Francesca. You know the rules.'

Frankie pulled out of his hold and got off the bed, snatching up a bathrobe, tying it vicious movements. 'Wow, you really know how to kill the mood.'

He swung his legs over the edge of the cabana bed and stood, not bothering to cover his nakedness. 'I don't want you to get any false hopes about me. I've been honest with you. Brutally honest.'

'You certainly have.' She didn't bother toning down the sarcasm in her tone. 'But what I am finding hard to understand is how we're going to go from this…' she waved her hand at the cabana bed where they had made passionate love '…to saying goodbye at the end of the year.' She snapped her fingers. 'Just like that.'

He compressed his lips until they momentarily disappeared. 'It will only be hard if we make it hard. We're adults. We can be civil about it. There's no need for either of us to be bitter.' He turned and went to the poolside bathroom and shut the door with a conversation-closed click.

But what if one of us is heartbroken?

Frankie couldn't ask it out loud. She didn't dare reveal how her feelings had undergone such a massive change. She had broken his rule. She had fallen in love with him. How could she not have fallen in love with a man who made love to her so exquisitely? Who listened to her, who made her feel safe enough to share her deepest secrets and insecurities? He had dismantled the ice cage around her heart with every kiss, every stroke, every caress. But it wasn't just his touch that had melted her. It was the quality of the man he was, the good man from a horrible background who had fought so valiantly to be something better than fate had planned.

She admired him, respected him. Adored him.

And in a year, according to his rules, she would lose him.

CHAPTER TWELVE

A WEEK OR so later, once they were back in Milan, Gabriel had to fly to Rome overnight to sign off on the billion-dollar business deal he was working on. Frankie was surprised, and a little hurt, that he hadn't asked her to accompany him, especially since he had married her to convince his corporate colleagues he was worthy of their trust. But ever since they had come back from Marseille she had sensed a subtle change in him. He was still just as passionate and attentive with his lovemaking, but he seemed even more preoccupied than usual.

She knew he was worried about his sister and worried about the business deal. But she couldn't help wondering if their conversation that night on their honeymoon, about his desire never to become a father, had triggered something in him. Something that made him fully present physically, but with a part of him—the emotional, feeling part she most wanted access to—locked away.

Gabriel's housekeeper had left for the day, and Frankie was settling down for a lonely night in front of the television in Gabriel's gorgeous villa in Milan when she heard the front door being unlocked and then footsteps as someone entered the house. She jumped off the sofa, wondering if Gabriel had changed his mind about staying overnight in Rome.

'Gabriel? Is that you?' She came out of the sitting room and encountered a slim young woman dressed entirely in black, with bleached blonde hair and eyes the same colour as Gabriel's.

'Carli?' Frankie said.

'*Sì.*' Carli's gaze assessed Frankie from head to foot in a way that could only be described as insulting. 'So. You're my brother's wife?'

'Yes…' Frankie offered her hand. 'I've been looking forward to meeting you…'

Carli ignored Frankie's hand and strode past to walk into the kitchen as if she owned the place. 'Where's Gabriel?' she tossed over her shoulder.

'He's in Rome. For business.' Frankie followed her, feeling like a servant attending to a snooty-nosed house guest. 'Can I make get you a drink? Something to eat? Maria has left for the day but she made some—'

'Do you love him?' Carli's gaze was as penetrating as a laser beam.

Frankie didn't have to hesitate with her answer. 'Yes. I do. Very much.'

Carli took an apple out of the fruit bowl on the bench and took a noisy bite, her eyes never leaving Frankie's face. 'I'm not going to like you just because you're married to him, you know.'

'I wouldn't expect you to,' Frankie said. 'But it would be nice for Gabriel if we were to become friends, don't you think?' Although she knew he wasn't keen on her becoming close to his sister, Frankie could sense an aura of loneliness and isolation surrounding Carli.

And didn't *she* know all about loneliness and isolation?

'Maybe.' Carli's look was so sceptical she could have worked for the FBI. Street-smart and highly intelligent, she reminded Frankie of a puppy that had been kicked too many times to ever come close to a human again. 'When's he coming back from Rome?'

'Tomorrow,' Frankie said. 'I'm sure he'd love to see you. Would you like to stay and—' Carli suddenly winced and clutched at her stomach. 'What's wrong? Are you unwell?'

Carli sucked in a breath. 'It's nothing.'

'But you don't look well at all. You're pale and sweaty and—'

'Do you have any painkillers? It's just bad period pain.' She winced again. 'Really bad.'

'Of course. I'll get something for you,' Frankie said. 'Why don't you come and lie down in one of the bedrooms and I'll get a hot pack for you. That usually helps me when I have mine…' She bit her lip and wondered with a jolt when her last period had been. She did a mental tally… Her stomach dropped like a boulder off a cliff.

She was late. A week late.

She tried not to panic and concentrated on getting Carli sorted. She had been late before. She had a wacky cycle, which was why she was taking the Pill. Had she somehow not absorbed a dose?

Frankie was glad of the distraction of taking care of Gabriel's sister. She couldn't think about the possibility of a pregnancy right now. She would get a test kit and make sure. She didn't even have to mention it to him. If it wasn't positive, then what would be the point? But the thought of a baby kept creeping back into her thoughts. It was sad to think Gabriel didn't have any future plans for fatherhood. Who else would she want to father her children? She couldn't imagine being with anyone else now. It wouldn't feel right to share her body with anyone but him.

It wouldn't be possible for her to love anyone but him.

Gabriel had planned to stay in Rome overnight but once his meeting with Alessandro De Angelo was over, all he wanted was to go home to be with Frankie. He had been preoccupied with this business deal, and he would be lying if he said his conversation with Frankie about fatherhood hadn't unsettled him. Not because he was going to change his mind.

He was not.

It was the niggling worry of the issue she had raised, of when it would be time to call the end to their marriage. He was finding it harder and harder to envisage a time when she wouldn't be in his bed.

In his life.

In his thoughts and feelings.

Yes, feelings—those messy things he took such great care to avoid.

But he had laid down the rules and he was going to stick to them. Perhaps by the time the year had rolled around, she would be sick of him. Ready to move on and take up with someone else. With someone who would marry her for a long time.

His gut soured at the thought of her with someone else. Jealousy—a feeling he was unfamiliar with—rose in him like bile. He suppressed it the way he suppressed every unwanted emotion. He stopped thinking about it. He slammed the lid of the trapdoor inside his head.

Bang. Shut. Locked.

Frankie had settled Carli in one of the guest rooms and taken up a hot pack and a packet of strong painkillers she had in her bag for the odd time she got severe period pain. She was a little conflicted about giving someone else her prescription medication, but she knew from experience how effective it was to break the pain cycle before it took hold. There was no point calling a doctor, even if Carli had agreed to it. Anyway, who did house calls for period pain? She gave Carli two tablets with a glass of water and left her to sleep.

Frankie had been downstairs about an hour when she heard the front door opening again. It was like *déjà vu* to go back out to the foyer, but this time it actually was Gabriel. 'Hi,' she said. 'I was just wondering whether to call you. I should have thought of it earlier. Your sister is here. She's sleeping upstairs.'

A frown snapped his brows together. 'How long has she been here?'

Frankie was a little hurt he hadn't come over to kiss her in greeting. His posture was stiff and guarded as if they were strangers meeting for the first time, not passionate lovers who knew every inch of each other's bodies. 'A couple of hours… maybe a bit more.'

'What was her mood like? Was she polite to you?'

'Not really but that's okay because she was in pain. I gave her some painkillers and—'

'What sort of painkillers?' His tone was as sharp as the crack of a whip.

Something cold and icy dripped in her stomach. 'Prescription ones. She had really bad period pain and I—'

'How many did you give her?' Every muscle on his face was tight with tension, his mouth set in a white line.

'Two.' Frankie was picking up a vibe that was making her heart race in panic. 'I left the packet with her...'

He let out a filthy curse and brushed past her, taking the stairs two at a time. Frankie followed him on legs that felt like soggy spaghetti. Her stomach was churning with nausea and she didn't know if it was because of her guilt over his sister or if she was indeed pregnant. She got to Carli's bedroom just in time to see Gabriel pick up the packet of medication. She held her breath as he took out the blister sleeves but thankfully all but four were gone. Frankie had taken two herself a few weeks ago. Relief swept through her in such a rush she felt light-headed...or maybe that too was because of Gabriel's baby growing inside her. *Gulp.*

Carli, meanwhile, was still sleeping as soundly as a kitten. She looked impossibly young and vulnerable lying there and Frankie's heart ached for all the suffering that had been in her life.

Gabriel gestured for them to leave Carli in peace and Frankie followed him out of the room. Once they were downstairs in the sitting room, he handed her the packet of painkillers. 'You'd bet-ter keep these under lock and key.' His tone had a chord of gravitas that matched his expression.

Frankie took the medication and slipped it into her pocket. 'I'm so sorry. I didn't think. I was wor-ried about her and—'

'Welcome to my world.' There was a weary in-flection in his voice. He scraped back his hair from his face, the lines of stress and strain far more no-ticeable than they had ever been before. 'She over-dosed once. Recently, just after your father died. Things had got on top of her. I can't be sure she won't do it again.'

'Oh, Gabriel…' Frankie closed the distance be-tween them and put her arms around his waist, resting her head against his chest. 'I can't imag-ine how dreadful it must be to always be worry-ing and watching out for her.'

He gave a long deep sigh and stroked the back of her head. 'Thanks for taking care of her. I'm sorry if she wasn't friendly towards you. She can be a bit funny meeting people for the first time. And the second and the third. Don't say I didn't warn you.'

Frankie lifted her head from his chest to glance up at him. 'It must be so hard for her. She's like you—sensitive and intelligent enough to know people will judge her no matter how hard she tries to fit in.'

He gave a lopsided smile and brushed a strand of hair away from her forehead. 'I missed you. That's why I came back early.'

Frankie's heart swelled like bread dough. Did that mean he was coming to care for her? 'I missed you too. Terribly.'

He lowered his mouth to hers in a long leisurely kiss that curled her toes and made a shiver race down her spine. He pulled back to look in her eyes. 'Time for bed?'

She smiled and linked her arms around his neck. 'Definitely time for bed.'

When Frankie woke the next morning, Gabriel was already downstairs, fixing breakfast for his sister. Carli was munching on a slice of ciabatta toast and scowling at him as if he had just delivered her a stern lecture. She looked across when Frankie came in and her scowl faded and was replaced by a sheepish smile. 'Hey, thanks for last night. Those pills really hit the spot. I didn't wake until half an hour ago. Best sleep I've had in ages.'

'You're welcome,' Frankie said. 'Do you feel better now?'

Carli rocked her hand back and forth. 'So-so. The first day is always the worst.'

'What are you plans, Carli?' Gabriel asked. 'I have to get to work soon. Do you need a lift anywhere or would you like to stay for a few days?'

Carli slipped off the stool she was perched on and dusted the crumbs off her hands. 'I'm meeting someone at ten but I'll walk. I need the exercise.'

Frankie could see the flicker of worry that flashed over Gabriel's features. 'And where will you stay tonight?' His tone was like that of a parent addressing a wayward teenager. 'And with whom?'

Carli rolled her eyes in a half circle and exchanged a *can-you-believe-what-I-have-to-put-up-with?* look with Frankie. 'Stop fussing like an old grandfather, Gabriel. I'm not going to go out and get myself pregnant.'

Frankie could feel her face flushing and quickly looked away on the pretence of pouring herself a cup of coffee from the freshly brewed pot Gabriel had prepared. Her heart was pounding with sickening dread. But then her hand stilled on the coffee pot, her heart pounding. Wasn't there a medical guideline for coffee to be avoided during pregnancy? Coffee and alcohol and soft cheeses…

'So, when are you two going to start having bambinos?' Carli asked.

There was a pregnant pause. *No pun intended.*

'We're not…in a hurry for that just yet,' Frankie said forcing herself to meet her inquisitive gaze.

Carli shrugged on her coat and lifted her hair out of the back of the collar. 'I reckon you'd make a good mum. Wouldn't she, Gabriel?'

Gabriel's expression was as unreadable as computer encryption. '*Sì*. An excellent mother.' He picked up his keys off the bench. 'Come on, Carli. I'll drop you off. I'm leaving now in any case.'

'Aren't you going to kiss your wife goodbye and tell her you love her?' Carli's tone was as cheeky as her sparkling gaze.

Gabriel came over to Frankie and lowered his mouth to hers in a brief kiss. 'I'll see you tonight, *cara*. I won't be late. We'll eat out.'

'You didn't say it,' Carli said. 'You didn't tell her you love her.'

'That's because Frankie already knows how I feel about her,' Gabriel said in an even tone. 'Don't you, *tesoro mio*?'

Frankie's smile felt as if it was stitched to her face. 'Yes. I do, and I feel exactly the same.'

CHAPTER THIRTEEN

FRANKIE CAME BACK to the villa half an hour later with a pregnancy test kit. She couldn't think straight unless she knew for sure. Had Gabriel's sister, in that street-smart way of hers, suspected something? Carli's question hadn't been an unreasonable one. Lots of newly married couples were asked the very same thing.

But Frankie and Gabriel were not just any other normal couple on the threshold of their life together. They only had a year together and that was not the sort of marriage in which she would like any child of hers to be born.

And yet the thought of a baby, a child of her own, was something that made her heart swell with excitement. She had been denied a mother but what if she became a mother herself? Showering her child with the love she had in her heart to give? It was all but bursting out of her—the joy and thrill of possibly holding a newborn baby in her arms in nine months' time.

Frankie performed the test and came out of the bathroom to wait the required time for the result. Her heart was beating like a kettle drum, the pounding in her chest reverberating in her skull. Was that two lines? Was that positive? There was a sound behind her and she swung around to see Gabriel standing there.

She whipped the test wand behind her back and forced a smile to her lips. '*Dio mio.* You startled me. W-why are you back so soon?' She was annoyed by the giveaway tremble in her voice. Even more annoyed by the storm of colour she could feel creeping over her cheeks.

His gaze narrowed in suspicion. 'What are you hiding?'

Frankie considered lying but she suspected he wouldn't fall for it anyway.

She swallowed against a pillow-sized lump in her throat and brought the test wand from behind her back. 'It's a pregnancy test. I—'

'What?' His voice was even more strangled than hers. 'You're…*pregnant*?' The horror in his expression didn't do anything favourable for her overstretched nerves.

'I—I don't actually know for sure…' Frankie looked at the wand, her heart in her throat. 'Oh… It's…negative…' She should have been feeling relieved but instead she felt strangely disappointed. Bitterly disappointed, as if she'd yet again jinxed someone's chance at life. First her mother, then her twin brother and now her little baby.

'Negative?' His gaze was so narrowly trained on hers he could have been aiming for a pistol target. 'Are you sure?'

'I'll do another test if you like.' Frankie gave him a self-deprecating glance. 'I have several.'

He scrubbed a hand down his face, the sound loud in the silence. 'How long have you suspected you were pregnant?' His voice had a scraped raw quality to it.

'Not long. I'm a week late and I—'

'But you've been taking the Pill, *sì*?' He sounded like a lawyer cross-examining a suspect in a major crime.

'Of course I have. How you could think otherwise?'

A glint of cynicism backlit his gaze. 'You were never a fan of my rules, were you?'

Frankie swung away in frustration and anger. 'You can't control everything in life, Gabriel. You think you can, but you can't. Sometimes medication can fail. Nothing is one hundred percent foolproof.' She turned and faced him again. 'Do you really think I would deliberately get myself pregnant to a man who only wants to be married to me for a year?'

'You know my reasons for that—'

'What *are* your reasons? You are an amazing brother to Carli. What makes you so sure you won't make a great father?'

Gabriel drew in a sharp breath and let it out in a savage rush. 'I don't want to talk about it.'

Frankie came up close and touched him on the arm but he took her by the shoulders and set her from him. 'No, Francesca. There's no point discussing this. I'm not going to change my mind.' He turned and walked out of the room as if he couldn't bear to be in the same room as her.

Frankie sat on the bed with a heavy sigh, her eyes straying to the pregnancy test wand. It was still negative. Her hand crept to her belly…thoughts of what could have been making her mood slump even further. She hadn't realised how much she longed to be a mother until it had been taken away. Was she so cursed that even the most natural thing in the world was to be denied her? She wanted a chance to hold her baby in her arms, to love it as she was sure her mother must have loved her. What if she never had a baby? What if she never had the chance to experience motherhood?

What if no one ever loved her the way she dearly longed to be loved?

Surely there was a way to get Gabriel to open up a little more about his reasons for avoiding fatherhood? Or was his intransigence about becoming a parent another way of keeping her at an emotional distance? He was prepared to enjoy the physical benefits of their marriage for a year but he was not prepared to share his deepest fears and misgivings about this most important of topics.

And that was the most heart-breaking thing of all—that he had so much to give but he was denying himself the opportunity to undo some of the damage of his past. He was denying himself love and family and, as a result, denying her as well.

For what future would she have without him?

Gabriel went for a walk to clear his head of images of tiny babies. To say he was shocked to find Frankie with a pregnancy test wand in her hand would be an understatement. Bringing a child into his life, having that child bear the surname of a criminal family such as his, was something he couldn't face. To have his child grow up and encounter the same prejudice and shame he had endured over the course of his life was unthinkable. He hadn't been able to save his brothers no matter how hard he'd tried. And his sister Carli was still an ongoing worry. His father was facing a lengthy prison sentence and the press would be all over the trial like ants at a picnic. How could he think about bringing a child into that mix?

The stain of Gabriel's background had never felt more indelible. He couldn't escape the shame of his heritage—it was never going to be whitewashed, no matter how much he wished it could be.

Because there was a secret place deep inside him that did wish it. The fatherhood trapdoor inside his head might be locked and bolted but every now and again a sliver of light would seep through. A beam of possibility, of hope that he could have a normal life. A life that included a wife who adored him and whom he adored in return. A family, children who looked for him for love and protection.

But nothing about him was normal.

It never had been and it never would be.

Frankie didn't see Gabriel until the following evening. He had sent her a text that something had come up at work but she suspected it had more to do with him needing some space. He hadn't slept with her the night before. She didn't even know if he had come back home at all. She refused to think of where he might have been or if anyone had been with him. She hated feeling those snapping jaws of jealousy nipping at her self-esteem but how could she feel secure when he kept putting up a wall?

It was hard for her to settle to anything. Ever since the pregnancy scare, she had felt on edge, unsettled, restless and empty. Empty of hope. She had thought she was doing the right thing in marrying Gabriel to save her heritage and her father's reputation. But at what personal cost? She was married to a man who had a clock ticking on their relationship. With rules he insisted could not be broken. What sort of relationship was that? Especially when she wanted more. Much more. The more she knew in her heart he was capable of giving, but was too stubborn or too closed down to admit it.

Gabriel came into the bedroom where she was preparing for bed. His expression reminded her of a tightly closed vault—barely a muscle moved, not even to smile. 'Sorry I'm late. I got caught up with something.'

Frankie folded her cardigan with exaggerated care and laid it over the back of the velvet wing chair. 'We need to talk. Really talk.'

A flash of anger lit his gaze. 'So, you're still insisting on hearing all the gory details of my childhood?'

'If you're ready to tell me, then yes.'

He rubbed a hand down his face as if he would like to erase the jagged white scar on his cheekbone. 'No one could come out of my family and not have baggage. I've prided myself on being the normal one in my family. But I'm not. I'm just as damaged, just as soiled as the rest of them.'

Frankie frowned. 'No, you're not, You're a wonderful person, Gabriel, and I—'

'Listen to me, Francesca.' His tone was so brittle it shocked her into silence. He took a harsh-sounding breath and continued. 'I have been educated on the proceeds of drugs, of other people's miserable suffering. I can never wipe that from my memory no matter how much I want to. I enjoyed every privilege that my father's filthy money could buy from the age of ten or so until I was hit in the face by the ugly truth.'

'But you didn't sell the drugs. You're not responsible for—'

'No, but I *feel* responsible.' His fist jabbed at his chest where his heart was situated. Jab. Jab. Jab. 'I feel it every time I see a homeless drug addict begging on the streets. I feel it every time I see a discarded syringe in a back alley. Damn it, I feel it every time I see sign my surname across a contract. That's who I am. A Salvetti. I can't escape it and I would rather die than let any child of mine bear the burden of that name and all the horror and suffering it represents.'

Frankie made a move towards him but he held up his hand like a stop sign.

'Nothing you can say will make me change my mind.' His tone was underlined with steel.

How could she reach him? How could she dismantle the fortress that imprisoned him? Or was she a fool for even wanting to try? Frankie took a steadying breath as the realisation hit her like a punishing slap. She knew what she had to do. A part of her had always known it would come to this sort of showdown. The clash of their worlds, their needs, their ghosts. 'Then there's no point in us continuing with our marriage.' She was surprised her voice came out as determined as his had done. Determined and yet defeated.

A flicker passed through his gaze like the twitch of a muscle. 'What are you saying?'

Frankie swallowed a thickening in her throat. 'I can't do this any more. I can't stay in a loveless marriage. Downstairs with Carli yesterday morning… Do you know how hard it was for me to lie to her? To act as if we're a loved-up couple who want to spend the rest of our lives together? I can't do it. I can't be a robot and turn off my feelings just because you insist on it. I want a normal life. I want a family. I want to be loved and give love in return. But you can't or won't do that for me so I have to leave.'

'Do you know what you will lose if you walk out on our agreement?' His features were etched in stone. Hard, unfeeling, impenetrable stone.

'I lost my family home a long time ago,' Frankie said on a ragged sigh. 'I lost it the day my mother and twin brother died. It's time for someone else to live there now. Someone who will fill it with love and joy and happiness. You and I aren't that couple. We never were.'

Gabriel strode to the other side of the room near the windows. His back was like a brick wall, every muscle pulled tight. 'This seems rather sudden.' He turned back to look at her, his expression so cold he could have been discussing an employee unexpectedly handing in their notice. 'Especially after the other night.' His gaze ran over her body as if he was mentally undressing her as he had done when he had made love to her so passionately.

Frankie stiffened her shoulders, embracing her anger because she would rather be angry than burst into tears. Better to show anger than to show how much she cared. That would be the ultimate in humiliation. 'Do you have to be so insulting?'

'I think it's reasonable for me to ask why you've suddenly decided to renege on our agreement.' His gaze glittered with resentment. 'Don't you think that's fair?'

'Life isn't fair, Gabriel. You of all people know that,' Frankie said in a weighty tone. 'I hope this doesn't jeopardise your business deal. Or upset your sister in any way.'

'What would you care about that?' His lips were so tightly compressed a slip of paper wouldn't have got through. 'One could even think you've planned this all along.'

'If that's what you really think of me, then my decision to leave is all the more warranted,' Frankie said, taking off her engagement and wedding rings and placing them on the chest of drawers. 'I'll leave in the morning for London. I hope you don't mind me spending one more night here? In the spare room, of course.'

'Of course.' His mouth had a cruelly mocking twist that made her heart give a painful spasm.

And without another word he walked out of the room and left her there, surrounded by her shattered hopes.

Gabriel couldn't face watching Frankie leave the next morning. He had spent a sleepless night, torn between blackmailing her to stay and the need to distance himself from a host of spiralling emotions he wasn't sure he could recognise, much less handle. He was disappointed in her decision, of course he was, but that didn't mean he was devastated or heartbroken. He didn't feel that depth of emotion for anyone. He didn't allow himself to. Would not allow himself to get so close to someone and then have them walk away.

Seeing Frankie with that pregnancy test in her hand had been like slamming into a wall at high speed. He had forgotten to take his wallet with him when he'd left with his sister. He didn't like to think too hard about how he would have felt if that test had been positive. Didn't he have enough worry about with his sister without taking on fatherhood?

The cold hard dread of finding Carli upstairs with a packet of narcotics next to her had almost given him a heart attack. That's what fatherhood would be like—the fear of not being there when your children needed you the most. Not being able to keep them out of danger. Not being able to keep them safe. Not being *good* enough. That was the world he would be entering and he wasn't interested.

Not one bit.

Frankie stayed in a hotel for a couple of weeks until she could organise a place to live. She had sold her apartment as soon as she'd found out about her father's debts. She had texted Gabriel to inform him of her whereabouts in case there was anything of a legal nature to see to. He had responded with such brevity and formality, it only reinforced her decision to leave their marriage. She wasn't able to go back to her job, because someone had already been appointed to her position, since she had requested a year's leave.

The days were long and lonely and the savage start to winter didn't lift her spirits. The rain and sleet fell like the tears she had shed in private. It was particularly heart-wrenching watching other couples going about their business. Huddled under a shared umbrella, dashing under cover into a cosy café to escape the weather. Holding hands across the table, gazing into each other's eyes as if no one else existed.

Frankie sat in the same café every day, it was a form of self-torture but she couldn't seem to help it. She was punishing herself for not being enough for Gabriel. For not being the perfect person—a person without a lifelong curse—to finally unlock his guarded heart. She wondered now if she should have told him she loved him. If she should have taken that chance, that impossibly slim chance to openly express her feelings.

But then she berated herself for even thinking there was a chance he might return them. Hadn't his tone and expression and body language told her everything she needed to know? He wasn't in love with her. She was nothing more than a cog in the machine of his wealth-making enterprise. In his attempt to rid himself of all his shameful background represented. Sure, it had been nice of him to offer to rescue her from financial ruin, but that had been because of his relationship with her father, not because of her. He was too ashamed of his past to open his heart to her or to anyone. He had let her go so easily. As if she had been a house guest who had overstayed their welcome.

And yet she wondered what he would have done if she had indeed been pregnant. But wasn't that why she had to leave? The longer she stayed with him the more she would crave what he insisted he could never give. What she wanted more than any-thing.

His love.

Gabriel came home from yet another brute of a day at work to find his sister parked in the sitting room with a pizza box open in front of her. He hadn't

seen or heard from her since Frankie had left and
he hadn't had the heart to tell his sister by phone
or text. He hadn't wanted to say it out loud or write
it. To hear those words, to see them in print would
be too much to bear.

It made it too permanent. Too painful.

He was still getting used to the silence. The
emptiness. The loneliness. Before Frankie had
come into his life, he had been happy in his own
company. Coming home after work had been a re-
spite after dealing with business and demanding
people and pressing deadlines. But now his villa
was like a cold and quiet museum once all the tour-
ists and security staff had left for the day. Even the
portraits and marble statues seemed to be passing
judgement on him, staring at him with accusing
eyes. *Why did you let her go?* The air seemed to
ring with their accusations, their disappointment—
the same disappointment he had in himself.

Disappointment and his old friend shame.

'Where's Frankie?' Carli asked.

He glowered at her and strode over to pour himself a stiff drink. 'Don't ask.'

She dropped the pizza slice as if it had suddenly
burned her. 'You mean she…left you?' Carli's expression was so gobsmacked he felt the perverse
need to congratulate himself on his acting ability.
He had done the husband-in-love gig so well he
was almost starting to believe it himself. Almost.

'Yep. And that's all I'm going to say on the subject so don't—'

'But that's crazy.' Carli jumped off the sofa and came over to him, frowning so hard her eyebrows met over her eyes. 'Why did you let her leave?'

Gabriel was starting to think it was a fair enough question to ask. Why had he let her go? He was miserable without her. He couldn't concentrate on anything. He couldn't eat or sleep. He was a walking zombie with an emptiness inside his chest that nothing would fill. And his office staff were all on the verge of walking out on him because of his foul temper. 'Look, I'd rather not talk about it.'

'Well, I *do* want to talk about it,' Carli said, planting her feet and crossing her arms. 'She's perfect for you, Gabriel. You know she is. I knew it as soon as I met her.'

'I thought you were rude to her when you first met?'

She shrugged as if that didn't matter. 'So? That's not the point. The point is she loves you. She told me.'

He let out a heavy sigh. 'It was an act. We were both acting. I paid off her father's debts in exchange for a year of marriage so I could nail an important business deal.'

Carli dropped her arms from her across her middle and put them on her hips instead, her expression scathing. 'You *what*?'

Gabriel grimaced. 'Yeah, well, I know it sounds a little clinical.'

'She wasn't acting, you know,' Carli said. 'And neither were you. You're just too blind to see it or too damn stubborn to admit it.'

Had he been too blind? Too stubborn? Gabriel wasn't used to acknowledging his feelings. He'd always shoved them aside, ignored them until they faded away. But they weren't fading now. They refused to be ignored. They were getting stronger, more insistent on being accepted and validated and celebrated. The emotions he had locked away were flooding into his chest so fast he could barely draw breath.

He had to go to Frankie to tell her how he felt. How he had felt right from the start. Wasn't that why he had waited four long years to claim her? But did she love him? Really love him? How could it be possible she could love him even half as much as he loved her?

Gabriel grasped his sister by the arms. 'Will you be all right if I go to London overnight? There's something I have to do.' He was surprised he got his voice to work without blubbering like a heart-sick fool.

'Of course I'll be all right,' Carli said, eyes suddenly sparkling. 'You have to stop worrying about me all the time. I have a nice boyfriend now. We met on the train a couple of weeks ago. He's stable and caring and I can't wait to introduce you. But not until you sort yourself out.'

'I can't help worrying about you, *mio piccolo*.' He gave her a bone-crushing hug and kissed the top of her head. 'I couldn't bear to lose you. You do know that, don't you?'

Carli pulled out of his hold and gave him a playful punch on the arm. 'Better hurry. Frankie might have fallen in love with someone else by now.'

Not if I can help it.

Frankie was doing her people-watching thing in her usual café. She had ordered a meal but she had barely touched it. She pushed the bowl of bouillabaisse away in disgust. What was she doing torturing herself with constant reminders of her time with Gabriel? She could barely think of him without a pain seizing her in the chest. She couldn't remember when she last slept more than a couple of hours without turning in the bed to search for him. The loneliness was weighing her down, dragging at her spirits, making ache from head to foot. She hadn't thought it possible that unrequited love could have such a physical as well as emotional effect on her. It was like a disease, taking every bit of energy and vitality out of her.

'May I join you?'

Frankie's head jerked up and she blinked to clear her vision. Was she imagining Gabriel standing next to the vacant chair on the opposite side of her table? 'How on earth did you know I was here?'

He gave a wry smile. 'You don't get to grow up in a criminal family without learning a few tricks on how to track down a target.'

Her lips were so dry she could barely move them to speak. 'But why are you here? I thought we said all that needed to be said back in Milan.'

He pulled out the chair and sat, his knees bumping hers under the table. He reached for her hands and encased them in his. 'I didn't say anywhere near what I should have said. I was a fool to let you go without telling you how much I love you.'

Frankie's heart kicked against her breastbone. 'You love me?'

His smile was so tender it made tears form in her eyes. 'I love you to distraction. You only have to ask my staff to know that. They're all threatening to walk out on me. And my sister. I've been so miserable without you, *tesoro mio*. You have no idea how miserable.'

'I think I do,' she said, gulping back a happy sob. 'I've been so lonely without you. I spend hours in this café torturing myself watching other couples and wishing I could be happy like them.'

'I will make sure you are happy from this day forward,' he said. 'Nothing will bring me greater satisfaction than making you happy for the rest of our lives.' He stood and pulled her to her feet, holding her in the circle of his arms, not one bit concerned the other diners were watching them with avid interest. 'Come back to me, *cara*. Please? Let's build a life together, a family.'

Her heart leapt again. 'Do you mean it? You want children?'

His eyes shone with moisture. 'I can live with the shame of my family's name. I can live with the shame of having half my family locked away in prison. But I can't live without you.' He smiled and continued. 'Anyway, I reckon I'll be a pretty awesome father. I've had plenty of practice, right? Just ask Carli.'

Frankie hugged him hard enough to pop a rib. 'Oh, darling, I can't believe it. I'm so happy I can barely express it.' She gazed up at him again. 'I was so disappointed when the pregnancy test was negative. All my life I've felt like I had a curse on me. My mother, my twin brother, my sad father who could never get his life back on track. The negative test seemed to be another confirmation of my failure.'

'You're not a failure,' Gabriel said. 'You're the most wonderful person in the world. The most perfect woman for me. I can't imagine loving anyone the way I love you. We will build a life together that will erase whatever sadness that has gone before. We will be a great team. I know it in my heart. The heart you and only you have the key to.'

Frankie wound her arms around his neck, standing on tiptoe to press her lips to his. 'I didn't think it was possible to love someone as much as I love you. Do you really love me? Please tell me I'm not dreaming this.'

'*Un centinaio di cuori non sabrebbero abbastanza per contenere tutto il motr per te,*' Gabriel said. 'A hundred hearts would be not enough to contain all my love for you.'

And his mouth came down to claim hers in a kiss that sealed his promise for ever.

* * * * *

If you enjoyed
Penniless Virgin to Sicilian's Bride
by Melanie Milburne
you're sure to enjoy these other
Conveniently Wed! stories!

My Bought Virgin Wife
by Caitlin Crews
The Sicilian's Bought Cinderella
by Michelle Smart
Crown Prince's Bought Bride
by Maya Blake
Chosen as the Sheikh's Royal Bride
by Jennie Lucas

Available now!

⬡ HARLEQUIN
™

Presents®

Available May 21, 2019

#3721 THE SHEIKH CROWNS HIS VIRGIN
Billionaires at the Altar
by Lynne Graham

When Zoe is kidnapped, she's saved by Raj—an exiled desert prince. The attraction between them is instant! Yet her rescue comes with a price: to avoid a scandal, Zoe *must* become Raj's virgin bride...

#3722 SHOCK HEIR FOR THE KING
Secret Heirs of Billionaires
by Clare Connelly

Frankie is shocked when Matt, the stranger she gave her innocence to, reappears. Now she's in for the biggest shock of all—he's actually *King* Matthias! And to claim his heir, he demands Frankie become his queen!

#3723 GREEK'S BABY OF REDEMPTION
One Night With Consequences
by Kate Hewitt

When brooding billionaire Alex needs a wife to secure his business, his housekeeper, Milly, agrees. But their wedding night sparks an unexpected fire... Could Milly—and his unborn child—be the key to Alex's redemption?

#3724 UNTOUCHED UNTIL HER ULTRA-RICH HUSBAND
by Dani Collins

To avoid destitution, Luli needs outrageously wealthy Gabriel's help. The multi-billionaire's solution? He'll secure both their futures by marrying her! But after sweeping Luli into his luxurious world, Gabriel discovers the chemistry with his untouched wife is *priceless*...

HPCNM0519RA

#3725 A SCANDALOUS MIDNIGHT IN MADRID
Passion in Paradise
by Susan Stephens

A moonlit encounter tempts Sadie all the way to Alejandro's castle...and into his bed! But their night of illicit pleasure soon turns Sadie into Spain's most scandalous headline: *Pregnant with Alejandro's baby!*

#3726 UNTAMED BILLIONAIRE'S INNOCENT BRIDE
Conveniently Wed!
by Caitlin Crews

To prevent a scandal, Lauren needs to find reclusive Dominik—her boss's estranged brother—and convince him to marry her! As Dominik awakens her long-dormant desire, will Lauren accept that their hunger can't be denied?

#3727 CLAIMING HIS REPLACEMENT QUEEN
Monteverre Marriages
by Amanda Cinelli

Khalil's motivation for marriage is politics, not passion. Yet a sizzling encounter with his soon-to-be queen, Cressida, changes everything. And the desire innocent Cressida ignites is too hot to resist...

#3728 REUNITED BY THE GREEK'S VOWS
by Andie Brock

Kate is stunned when ex-fiancé, Nikos, storms back into her life—and demands they marry! Desperate to save her company, she agrees. But what these heated adversaries don't anticipate is that their still-smoldering flame will explode into irresistible passion...

YOU CAN FIND MORE INFORMATION ON UPCOMING HARLEQUIN® TITLES, FREE EXCERPTS AND MORE AT WWW.HARLEQUIN.COM.

HPCNM0519RB

You told me what you were worth, Luli. Act like you believe it.

She had been acting. The whole time. Still was, especially as a handful
of designers whose names she knew from Mae's glossy magazines behaved
with deference as they welcomed her to a private showroom complete with
catwalk.

She had to fight back laughing with incredulity as they offered her
champagne, caviar, even a pedicure.

"I—" She glanced at Gabriel, expecting him to tell them she aspired to
model and should be treated like a clotheshorse, not royalty.

"A full wardrobe," he said. "Top to bottom, morning to night, office to
evening. Do what you can overnight, then send the rest to my address in
New York."

"Mais bien sûr, monsieur," the couturier said without a hint of falter in
her smile. "Our pleasure."

"Gabriel—" Luli started to protest as the women scattered.

"You remember what I said about this?" He tapped the wallet that held
her phone. "I need you to stay on brand."

"Reflect who you are?"

"Yes."

"Who are you?" she asked ruefully. "I only met you ten minutes ago."

"I'm a man who doesn't settle for anything less than the best." He
touched her chin. "The world is going to have a lot of questions about why
we married. Give them an answer."

His words roused the competitor who still lurked inside her. She wanted to prove to the world she was worthy to be his wife. Maybe she wanted to prove her worth to him, too. Definitely she longed to prove something to herself.

Either way, she made sure those long-ago years of preparation paid off. She had always been ruthless in evaluating her own shortcomings and knew how to play to her strengths. She might not be trying to win a crown today, but she hadn't been then, either. She'd been trying to win the approval of a woman who hadn't deserved her idolatry.

She pushed aside those dark memories and clung instead to the education she had gained in those difficult years.

"That neckline will make my shoulders look narrow," she said, making quick up-and-down choices. "The sweetheart style is better, but no ruffles at my hips. Don't show me yellow. Tangerine is better. A more verdant green. That one is too pale." In her head, she was sectioning out the building blocks of a cohesive stage presence. Youthful, but not too trendy. Sensual, but not overtly sexual. Charismatic without being showy.

"Something tells me I'm not needed," Gabriel said twenty minutes in and rose to leave. "We'll go for dinner in three hours." He glanced to the couturier. "And return in the morning for another fitting."

"Parfait. Merci, monsieur." Her smile was calm, but the way people were bustling told Luli how big a deal this was. How big a deal Gabriel was.

The women took her measurements while showing her unfinished pieces that only needed hemming or minimal tailoring so she could take them immediately.

"You'll be up all night," Luli murmured to one of the seamstresses.

The young woman moved quickly, but not fast enough for her boss, who kept crying, *"Vite! Vite!"*

"I'm sorry to put you through this," Luli added.

"Pas de problème. Monsieur Dean is a treasured client. It's our honor to provide your trousseau." She clamped her teeth on a pin between words. "Do you know where he's taking you for dinner? We should choose that dress next, so I can work on the alterations while you have your hair and makeup done. It must be fabulous. The world will be watching."

She would be presented publicly as his wife, Luli realized with a hard thump in her heart.

Don't miss
Untouched Until Her Ultra-Rich Husband.
Available June 2019 wherever
Harlequin® Presents books and ebooks are sold.

www.Harlequin.com

HPEXP0519

Want to give in to temptation with
steamy tales of irresistible desire?

Check out **Harlequin® Presents®,
Harlequin® Desire** and
Harlequin® Kimani™ Romance books!

New books available every month!

CONNECT WITH US AT:

Facebook.com/groups/HarlequinConnection

Facebook.com/HarlequinBooks

Twitter.com/HarlequinBooks

Instagram.com/HarlequinBooks

Pinterest.com/HarlequinBooks

ReaderService.com

**ROMANCE WHEN
YOU NEED IT**

PGENRE2018